Leonard Kearon, MSc, was born and raised in Waterford City, Ireland. He graduated from Waterford Institute of Technology with a Master of Science. His strong love of history inspired him to write history leaflets for various locations in Waterford City as well as his first book, *The Saga of the Déise*. His strong love of comics, anime, manga along with ancient mythology inspired him to write *The Legend of Circe: Circe's Awakening*.

Leonard Kearon MSc

THE LEGEND OF CIRCE: CIRCE'S AWAKENING

AUSTIN MACAULEY PUBLISHERS™

LONDON • CAMBRIDGE • NEW YORK • SHARJAH

A CIP catalogue record for this title is available from the British Library.

ISBN 9781528971034 (Paperback)
ISBN 9781528971201 (ePub e-book)

www.austinmacauley.com

First Published 2023
Austin Macauley Publishers Ltd®
1 Canada Square
Canary Wharf
London
E14 5AA

Thanks must be paid to the following people. First my family; my parents, William and Yvonne, and my brother Joseph for their continuous support in this and my other projects.

I would also like to thank my extended family of uncles, aunts and cousins who kept being interested in the creation of this book and assuring me that I would have a good number of customers when this book would finally be published

Finally, I would like to thank you, the reader, for reading this book.

Table of Contents

Chapter 1
Let's Meet Our Heroine

The city of Sunsport, a beautiful historical city situated on the South-East coast of Hibernia. With clean flowing rivers and a strange mix of modern and historical buildings, Sunsport is a prime location for people to live, tourists to visit and alien robots to invade…

"General, we have arrived above the beachhead, shall we proceed?" Captain Razor asked.

"The word is given, and this world will be taken by the Cybertrix Sphere!" General Cybertrix proclaimed.

The Cybertrix Sphere is a powerful robotic empire dedicated to wiping out all inferior organic life. Earth was their next target and Sunsport was chosen the beachhead.

On the streets, panic set in as the skies filled with alien ships and thousands of black, humanoid robots with a red V-shaped visor for eyes and gun arms flew down from the ships. Some people ran into the nearby shops, others foolishly decided to record the aliens with their phones, and some were excited to see the aliens.

"Weheheheheheheheh! Cool aliens!" said one prat.

"Yeah! Maybe they will trash the school," another prat said.

Away from the prats, a young woman called Circe Goodwin was trying to escape the alien attack. Her green eyes were filled with terror like so many other people and things got worse when the Cybertrix Sphere Soldiers started firing. Lasers rained down in every direction during the chaos, Circe saw a child fall. As she tried to help the child, a soldier flew towards her. Instinctively, she tried to shield the child, just then the soldier exploded.

Circe and the child looked up, standing in front of them was Elemental, one of Sunsport's heroes, she was joined by her husband, Hyperdrive. Elemental stood there with her long ash-blonde and black hair wearing a black and gold costume. Hyperdrive, looked like a knight wearing red and silver armour and armed with an energy sword and shield.

"So much for our romantic picnic," Elemental said, looking at the alien attack.

"Don't worry, Lizzie, we'll defeat these in no time and then have that picnic," Hyperdrive said confidently.

"You two better get to safety," Elemental said to Circe and the child.

"Okay!" Circe said, a bit surprised that a hero had talked to her. "Come on, let's hide in here and then find your parents."

Elemental took to the sky and started creating wind gust that caused the soldiers to smash into each other. Hyperdrive used his armour's rocket jets to speed around any of the soldiers that his wife missed and destroy them with his sword. Soon other heroes arrived on the scene, and soon the alien invasion was over.

When the heroes declared it safe, everyone appeared from the shops and buildings. There was some destruction and a number of injuries but thankfully no fatalities. As the news crews talked the heroes, Circe and the child began to look for the child's parents. Suddenly, the two heard a shout as the child's parents appeared and rushed towards them.

"Thank you for finding our child!" The mother said, having feared the worse.

"It was nothing," Circe said modestly.

"She was really brave, mommy, she protected me from a bad robot and then Elemental stopped the bad robot." The child said excitedly as Circe blushed slightly.

"How can we ever thank you!" The father said, hugging his child.

"Just knowing you are all safe and reunited is enough," Circe said, not wanting the attention. Suddenly her phone rang.

"Excuse me," she said politely as she answered her phone. "Hi, Dad! Yeah, I'm fine. Do you want me to get the milk still? It's okay, the shops are all open still. I'll get the milk and head on home."

She looked at the happy family and smiled. "I have to go; my Dad is worrying about me."

"Wait, before you go, what's your name?" The mother asked.

"Circe, Circe Goodwin," she replied with a smile before leaving.

A short time later, Circe had crossed one of Sunsport's two main bridges and made her way home to Saint Declan's Castle. Saint Declan's Castle was a castle that stood on top of a hill overlooking the city. The castle was now a boarding school but unlike the other students, Circe lived there permanently with her dad, David who was the janitor there.

She entered through the main doors into the great hallway. A massive staircase rose in front of her which led to the student's rooms and some of the classrooms. The majority of the school was on the ground floor. Circe headed past the staircase and towards a grandfather's clock past the library. She took out a set of keys and placed a long key into a keyhole next to the clock. A quick turn and the grandfather clock moved, she pulled it to reveal a passageway.

As she entered the passageway which made sure to close the door behind her. She walked down the passageway which was well lit and full of photos of herself and her dad. At the end of the passageway, she arrived at another door, she used the smaller key to open it which led to her home. The place was quite small, there was a small hall which led to a kitchen/dining room, two bedrooms, a living room, and a bathroom. There was also a door that led to the back of the school which included her dad's garden.

"Dad, I'm home!" she shouted.

"Are you okay?" Her dad appeared from the kitchen and quickly gave her a huge hug, lifting her off the ground.

"Yeah Dad, I'm fine, it isn't the first time one of us has been caught in one of these attacks."

"Just because it happens doesn't mean I will stop worrying about your safety. You know that," he said, relieved.

"I know, and can you put me down before I drop the milk," she spoke.

"Oh sorry."

David put his daughter down and the two went into the kitchen/dining room. Circe placed the milk in the fridge as her dad started making sandwiches.

"Your birthday's coming up soon, any ideas what you want?"

Presents were always tricky to buy. It wasn't what you wanted; it was what the other could afford. There was something she wanted, but she was afraid to ask as her father would try and dodge it.

"What's the budget?" She asked politely.

"Would €50 be, okay?" her dad replied.

He wished he didn't have to set a budget, Circe meant everything to him, and he wanted her to be happy but working as a janitor for a boarding school wasn't exactly a high paying job. The dean did his best to make sure they could pay him a decent wage.

"That will be fine, Dad," she said with a smile.

"Are you sure?"

"I'm sure. Though there is something I would like…" She said, almost afraid to say what she wanted.

"What is it? It will be hard to get you anything if you don't tell me," her dad said, half joking and half worried that he knew what was coming next.

"I would like know more about how you adopted me," Circe said, already regretting saying it.

"Circe…" He said with a heavy sigh.

"Dad, I have a right to know, don't I?" She asked sweetly.

"Of course, you do, it's just I'm afraid what will happen if I tell you," he said, concerned.

"I understand, but I really want to know and every other time I have brought it up, you avoid the subject. I love you Dad, what you tell me won't change that, I'm going to be seventeen, I just want to know why you adopted me," Circe said, almost pleading.

"I adopted you, because I love you," He said, it was the truth, but he knew Circe wanted more.

"Dad, if you don't want to tell me…" Circe said, almost getting upset.

"Circe, I'm just trying to protect you," he said but not wanting to upset his daughter or keep the truth from her, so with a heavy sigh, "but you deserve to know, so I will tell you all on your birthday."

"You will?!" she said as her eyes lit up, "Oh thank you!" she quickly hugged her dad.

"Just remember, you may not like what you learn," her dad warned her.

That night, Circe was lying in her bed, wondering if she made the right decision. She was finally going to learn about her adoption but why was her dad afraid of telling her? Was he afraid she would leave him to try and find her biological parents? It was possible, but she would never do that, he was her dad, who raised her and loved her. Was there some dark secret he was hiding? If that were the case, he wouldn't tell her. Maybe talking about her adoption would bring up a lot of bad memories for her dad? No, he was concerned about her not himself. Maybe her adoption is a sad tale? It was possible, still she was going to find out, but that wouldn't be for a while. Tomorrow was a school day, so she better stop thinking and get some sleep.

The next morning, Circe was getting dressed for school while listening to the radio.

Now on Blast FM, after Sunsport was attacked by robots and saved by some of the heroes, we are asking our listeners, if you were a hero what powers would you have? John has texted us, saying he would love to have the power to create food from thin air, so he would never be hungry. I'm not sure it would be that useful a power…"

She turned off the radio and made sure her uniform was okay and headed to the living room where her dad was typing on his laptop.

"Did you sleep well last night?" David asked.

"I did, also since today is a half-day, I was wondering if it would be okay, if I go into town with some of the girls, maybe get some ideas for a present?"

"As long as you don't get too much homework, you can."

"We shouldn't, the only classes today are double history which Mrs Hearne is doing to talk about history and mythology and then there is double art."

"What are you going to do about dinner, are you and the girls going to get something here or are you going to get something in town?"

"We hadn't decided yet, what are you planning to cook for the school dinner today anyways?" Circe wondered.

"As always here's the menu preview," Her dad said, printing off the menu he had just finished typing and handing it to her.

"Thanks, everyone keeps asking me what's for dinner."

"They can't wait until breakfast to see, can they?"

"No, they can't. Chicken Kiev, Beef Burger, Vegetarian Lasagne all served with Chips or Potatoes with Vegetables. Dessert is apple tart and cream. Sounds good."

"Thanks, well we better get going we don't want to be late," he said with a smile. "Don't forget your tie."

Circe quickly put on her uniform's tie, "I hate this, it always feels like a noose."

The two headed down the corridor to the school. David pushed open the grandfather clock and the two entered the school's main hall. Already it was buzzing with students, David hugged his daughter as he headed to the school's canteen while Circe headed meet up with her friends. Sitting on a bench were her friends Fiona Fitzpatrick, Claire Power and Yu Walsh.

"Hi Circe!" Fiona said, happy.

"Hi FiFi! Hi Claire! Hi Yu!" Circe said, excited.

"So, are you coming shopping with us?" Fiona asked.

"Yeah, my Dad said it was okay."

"That's great, still we haven't decided what we are going to do about dinner," Claire said.

"What's for dinner anyway Circe?" Yu asked as a crowd gathered to hear.

"Seriously, you guys can't wait until my Dad opens the canteen for breakfast?" Circe said, noticing the crowd, it was bad enough there was a large number of students but there was also a number of teachers as well.

"Sorry Circe, but we all love your Dad's food, and we are an impatient lot," Fiona said with a smile.

"Okay, today's menu is Chicken Kiev, Beef Burger, Vegetarian Lasagne all served with Chips or Potatoes with Vegetables. Dessert will be apple tart and cream," Circe said as everyone listened with bated breath.

As the crowd began to break up, all seemingly happy with the menu. Circe breathed a sigh of relief.

"So, staying in for dinner or go out?" She asked her friends.

"Well, the menu sounds really good, and it would be a lot cheaper than going into town for something," Fiona said carefully thinking.

"Also, there is apple tart! You know how much I love apples," Claire said, excited.

"Yeah, we know, also the less we spend on food, the more we have for shopping," Yu said, making a good point.

"So, it's settled we will get something to eat here and then go into town for some shopping," Fiona said as the other girls agreed.

Eventually, school was over, and the girls headed to the canteen for dinner. The canteen was packed as always and there was already a queue.

"Oh great, how come no matter what time we arrive there is already a queue?" Fiona said, annoyed.

"It must be my Dad's cooking, at least the line is moving," Circe said, trying to look on the bright side.

"What if they run out of apple tart before we get there?" Claire said, worried.

"Then you'll just have to wait until we get into town," Yu said jokingly.

"But you know the stuff in town isn't as nice," Claire said, still worried.

Eventually Circe and her friends reached the food. It all looked so good; David was there serving the students.

"Hello girls, what can I get you today?" David said with a smile.

"Hi Dad, can I have the chicken Kiev with chips and veg please?" Circe said politely.

"Of course, what would you like Fiona?" he said happily preparing his daughter's dinner.

"I'll take a beef burger with chips please," Fiona said, already looking forward to it.

"No problem, and for you Claire?"

"Do you have any apple tart left?"

"Apple tart, for dinner?" David said, surprised.

"I just want to make sure you aren't going to run out," Claire said, slightly embarrassed.

"Don't worry, I have plenty, so do you want apple tart for dinner or something else?" he said with a reassuring smile.

"That's good to hear, I'll have the chicken Kiev with potatoes please," Claire said, relieved.

"Coming right up, and for Yu?"

"Can I get the Vegetarian Lasagne?" Yu politely asked.

"Of course, you can."

Soon, all four girls had their dinners, which they paid for and then some seats. The canteen was packed but somehow there was always free seats around. As the four started eating, the topic of Circe's birthday and their shopping trip arose.

"So, are you looking forward to your birthday?" Fiona asked.

"Of course, this one is going to be really special," Circe said, excited.

"How come?" Claire asked taking another bite.

"Well… my Dad is finally going to me, how I was adopted," Circe said, part worried and part excited.

"Really, after all this time?" Yu said, surprised.

"Yeah, I have to admit, I am both nervous and excited," Circe said.

"How come? You wanted to know for ages," Fiona said.

"Yeah, but what if I learn something horrible?"

"Trust me Circe, from a fellow adoptee, nothing is worse than not knowing anything," Yu said.

"So, how did you react when your parents told you?" Circe asked.

"To be honest, it was as I expected. I had already guessed that I was adopted given I was Chinese, and my parents weren't, and they adopted me since they couldn't have kids of their own. Of course, your story could be different," Yu said.

"That's what worries me. My dad has always avoided telling me, it makes me wonder why he hasn't told me yet, despite me knowing I was adopted for years."

"At least, you are going find out," Fiona said.

"That's true."

The girls finished their dinner and Claire managed to get some apple tart. With no more school for the day. The four girls decided to change out of their uniforms before heading into the city. The four decided to walk into town since with was a nice day. After about fifteen minutes, they had arrived in the city centre.

"So, has your dad given you a budget for your present?" Fiona asked.

"Yeah, €50," Circe said, slightly embarrassed that she had to tell her friends that she had a budget, but they all understood.

I'm sure we will find something," Claire said, excited.

"Not to mention, we will need to look for presents for Circe ourselves," Yu reminded the others.

"Remember it doesn't have to be expensive or big," Circe said.

"We know!" her friends all said together.

Sunsport had a huge selection of shops, everything from clothes, books, film and music to toys and jewellery. The girls were spoiled for choice, checking out each shop hoping to get ideas.

"Do you have anything in mind?" Fiona asked.

"Well, I was thinking of maybe a party dress, something I could wear for special occasions and the like," Circe said thinking out loud.

"That sounds like a great idea," Fiona said.

"Now, can we find something that looks good and doesn't break the budget," Circe said, concerned.

"Don't fret, we'll find something," Claire said reassuringly.

"Yeah, now we have an idea, we are bound to get something," Yu said, buzzing with energy.

With a new focus, the girls hit all the clothes shops. In one clothes shop, they found a large number of party dresses. After ruling out any that were too expensive, Circe was glad there were still a good selection.

"Well, they are all the ones within the budget, hopefully there might be one I like," she said, looking though the dresses.

"How about this one?" Fiona said with a grin on her face as she took out a very skimpy dress.

"You are kidding me! My dad would kill me if I wore that!" Circe said, horrified.

"Relax, I'm only messing with you. To be honest, I'm not sure who would wear this?" Fiona said, looking at the dress again.

"This one look nice," Claire said, looking at a nice blue dress.

"Shame it's blue. I hate blue dresses," Circe said.

"Oh yeah, I forgot," Claire said.

It was starting to seem hopeless, when Circe spotted a lovely looking fuchsia dress with gold trim. She took it off the rack to have a better look.

"What do you think?" she asked her friends as she held it up to her body to get an idea of the length.

"It looks beautiful, try it on!" Fiona said.

Circe quickly took the dress to the dressing room and tried it on. She already liked the fit and the length was just what she liked, above the knee but not too short and while strapless, it wasn't exposing her cleavage. She looked at herself in the mirror and modelled a bit. The more she wore it the more she liked it. Hopefully, her friends would like it. She appeared from the dressing room and shown it off to her friends.

"What do you think?" She said, giving a twirl.

"That looks amazing, Circe!" Fiona said, amazed.

"I love it" Claire gushed.

"I have to admit, I'm a bit jealous" Yu said.

"I'm glad you like it," Circe said.

"What do you think Circe?" Fiona asked.

"I love it, now I just hope my Dad approves, after all he will be buying it," Circe said, hoping that her dad would approve. She headed back into the dressing room and changed back.

"When will your dad be able to go into town?" Yu asked.

"Hopefully tomorrow, oh what if someone else buys it before he can see it?" Circe started to worry, that she might lose the dress.

"Oh dear, couldn't you ask your dad to come in now?" Fiona asked.

"I don't know, I could try," Circe said as she quickly took out her phone and rang her dad.

"Hello honey, is everything okay?" David said, concerned, over the phone.

"Hi Dad, everything is okay, I was just wondering if you could come into the city for a bit, I've found the perfect birthday present," Circe said, hoping to convince her dad to come in.

"It can't wait until tomorrow?"

"It might be gone tomorrow, don't worry it is in budget and it would mean you won't have to be worrying about getting me a present."

"Okay, give me a few minutes and I'll be in. Where are you?"

"I'm in Darres Boutique."

"Okay, I'll see you there"

Circe waited in the store, while her friends decided to check out some other stores to get ideas for their presents. She waited impatiently hoping that no-one else would buy the dress before her dad came. After what seemed like an eternity, her dad finally arrived.

"So, where's this present that couldn't wait," he said with a smile.

Circe quickly ran over and showed her Dad the dress. He could clearly see she was excited about it. He looked at it, checked the price, looked at it again and started to make a lot of thinking noises. This was starting to worry Circe, maybe he didn't like it or maybe he was just messing, sometimes it was hard to tell.

"Put it on and I'll decide," he spoke.

Circe ran to the dressing room and put on the dress. She appeared from the room and showed it off to her Dad.

"Well? What do you think?" She said nervously.

Her Dad just looked at her and made some more thinking noises. After a while he said in a stern manner.

"Take it off, Circe."

Circe didn't like the tone. Did he hate it? She returned to dressing room and put back on her own clothes. Before she headed out, she looked at the dress one last time, was she not going to get it? She appeared for the dressing room with the dress in her hand.

"That's better," her dad said still with a stern tone. He noticed Circe expression as he took the dress of her.

"Well, I can't pay for it if you were still wearing it," he then said with a jovial tone.

Circe's eyes lit up.

"You mean it?" She said, delighted.

"Of course, I was only messing with you honey," he said, rubbing her ash-blonde hair.

"That wasn't funny," she said as she fixed her hair.

"Sorry," he said as he headed to the till. Soon the dress was in a bag and paid for.

"Remember, you have to wait until your birthday now," he said, keeping a tight hold on the bag.

"I know, thanks Dad," she said, giving her a hug.

As they were about to leave, a group of five teenagers entered the shop. They were the Puff Anders, Sam, Nicky, Andy, Kelly, and Eddie. They wore matching snake skinned tracksuits with hoods and started to smoke in the shop.

"Hey, you can't smoke in here!" the cashier shouted.

"We are the Puff Anders; we can smoke were we want," Sam said, taking another puff on his cigarette.

The cashier tried to stop them; but Nicky shoved her to the ground. David helped her up as the others laughed before each taking another puff. The smoke was getting irritating and caused Circe to cough.

"Hey, looks like someone doesn't our smoking," Andy said, noticing Circe.

"How rude!" laughed Kelly who then pushed Circe into a rack of clothes.

"Circe!" David shouted, concerned about his daughter's safety. The Puff Anders just laughed.

"What should we do know?" Eddie asked.

"Let's trash the place, since they don't seem to like us" Sam said with an evil grin.

"NO!" Circe shouted as a blast of Fuchsia energy shot out of her hands, hitting Sam which sent the Puff Ander through the window. The other Puff Adders looked in horror before fleeing out of the shop.

"Circe?" David asked concerned.

"Dad?" she said, scared as she saw Fuchsia smoke coming from her hands. "What's happened to me?"

Chapter 2
Surviving the Experience

Night had fallen in Sunsport and at St. Declan's Castle, David was having a hard time sleeping. He quietly stood in the doorway of his daughter's room and looked at his daughter sleeping peacefully. Today, gave him quite a fright, what had happened to his daughter? The doctors couldn't find anything wrong with her but firing energy blasts from your hands isn't normal. Did this have something to do with her real parents? Where are they going to take her away? Circe meant everything to him, he didn't want to lose her, but he didn't know what to do.

The morning sun vanquished the horrible night and Circe was checking the post. She was trying not to think of what happened yesterday, but it was hard not to. What if she fired at her friends or her dad? What was going to happen to her? Does her dad still love her? She shook her head to try and get the thoughts out and returned with the post.

"Anything?" her dad said.

"It's Saturday, so it mostly takeaway menus. Except for this…" Circe said, looking at an envelope addressed to her.

"Strange, I got everything out of post-box yesterday. So, it wasn't left there."

"It looks official, whatever it is" Circe said.

"Well open it," David said.

Circe carefully opened the envelope and took out the letter.

"It's from the Department of Superpowers and Heroics," Circe said, worried.

"What does it say?" her dad said, concerned.

"Dear Ms Goodwin, Due to your display of unregistered powers, you are required to attend an information meeting on Sunday at 2 p.m. Please come to the place where Russian Dragons and the Wings of Freedom guard the sounds of the people," Circe said as she read the letter.

"They put a riddle into an official letter?" her dad said, confused.

"They did, still Dad what does this mean?" Circe said as she started to get upset.

"Apparently they learned about your little display at the shop and want to talk about it" He said, reading the letter, before calming her down. "Circe, I'm as confused as you are about what has happened, but no matter what I'll help you as best as I can."

"Thanks Dad, that means a lot," she said, hugging her dad.

"I know, now let's figure out this riddle," he said, looking again at the letter, "Well, the Wings of Freedom is the name of the fountain in the park. Everyone knows that."

"That's true, wait aren't the cannons in the park from Russia or near there?" Circe said, thinking out loud.

"They are, so the place they are talking about is…"

"The bandstand!"

"It has to be," David said, rubbing her head.

"Dad!" she said as she fixed her hair.

The two then decided to figure out what to do for the information meeting and tried to enjoy the rest of their Saturday. The next day, the two headed to the park, as it was a beautiful sunny day, there were plenty of people around. The children's playground was full of kids and their parents trying to keep them under control. There were people walking their dogs or going for a jog, some people were even having picnics.

"It's been a while since we were here," said David.

"Yeah, it's sort of a shame when you think about it. Maybe we should come here when I'm haven't been summoned," Circe said, admiring the park.

"Maybe you still have bad memories of when you fell and cut your knee."

"That was years ago, and I got over that... eventually," Circe said with a smile.

The two made their way to the bandstand, however as they arrived Circe stopped for a moment.

"Dad, what's that?"

"What's what?" He said, confused.

"It almost looks like a building over near the Cycle track," she said, startled.

"No there's nothing there, maybe it is just the way the sun is shining."

"Maybe," she said as put whatever she saw out of her head and checked her phone to see the time.

"About ten minutes to go, still it is strange to have a meeting here."

"Yeah, it isn't very private, also how will whoever we are supposed to meet know who we are," David said, looking around.

"Well, the letter was written by Professor Fargo Jones, maybe he's going to meet us," Circe said, looking at the letter.

"Maybe, but unless he has a photo of you, it might be very difficult for him to find you."

As they waited, a young lady the same age as Circe with long blonde hair which was styled to cover her left eye arrived near the bandstand. She looked around and noticed Circe had the same letter she did.

"Excuse me," She asked politely, "Are you here for the information meeting?"

"I am" Circe replied.

"That's good, I thought I had missed it" The young lady said with a sigh of relief.

"Do you know anything about it? My Dad and I haven't a clue"

"Very little, I am guessing it's an introduction meeting for people who have developed powers or want to be a hero."

"I see, oh I'm Circe and this is my Dad, David," Circe said, introducing herself.

"I'm Alex, I've never heard the name Circe before" The young woman said, introducing herself.

"It's Greek," Circe said.

"So, you're Greek?"

"Ah No, I'm Hibernian and so is my family."

"I think it's a nice name."

"Thanks, by the way are you here with your parents?"

"No, my parents are busy, so I had to come on my own."

"Oh, by the way have we meet? You look familiar."

"No, we haven't," Alex said, sounding a bit nervous.

Suddenly a voice rang out.

"Attention could everyone who is attending the Information meeting please gather in front of the Bandstand."

Circe, David, and Alex headed to the Bandstand where there were a number of people and their parents waiting. Just in front of the bandstand was a youngish man with a cane.

"Greetings everyone, I'm Professor Fargo Jones, if you could all follow me" He said as he led the group into the bandstand.

Before any could question him, he pressed on a ring he was wearing and suddenly everything changed. There was a massive building where the cycling track used to be and stuff like the playground and other parts of the parks were gone and replaced with strange buildings and objects.

"Where have you taken us?!" One of the parents yelled as he grabbed Professor Fargo.

"Please there is no need for violence, I have taken you all to Sunsport Super School or S^3!" Professor Fargo said calmly.

"Say, what?!" The parent said as he let go.

"Sunsport Super School is a place where people with powers and/or a desire to become a hero can train without worrying about endangering the general public. Of course, the school is empty since it is a Sunday, so it is the perfect time to show you all around."

"But where are we? What happened to the Park?" Circe asked.

"Ah yes. The school and the surrounding area is in a different plane of existence that the rest of the city. It's a combination of magic and science. I could bore you with the details, but we will be here all day."

It was clear that no-one really understood what Professor Fargo said, but everyone decided to pretend they did so the tour could continue.

"The massive building you see here is the main school, where you will learn about the rules and regulations of having powers along with being trained in hero theory. The area outside the school is where the practical training happens. This may be on another plain of existence, but we don't want holes in our buildings."

"Do we have to sign up?" a very handsome young boy asked.

"It's not mandatory but the Department of Superpowers and Heroics would prefer your cooperation. Trying to use your powers or be a hero without training could result in you injuring innocent people, which could result in lawsuits. Unless you are planning to be a villain."

"Ah no sir."

"Good, now if you would all follow me inside, there is some paperwork that needs to be filled out."

Everyone groaned, no-one likes to fill in paperwork.

"Don't worry, it won't be too much," Professor Fargo reassured.

The Professor led everyone inside, where there were a couple of forms on a desk. Everyone took one of the forms and a pen and began to fill out the form. For the most part the form was easy, however one part of the form stumped everyone.

"Professor Fargo?" Alex asked concerned, "What are we supposed to put in the 'powers' category?"

"Don't worry about that, that section will be filled in when your powers/abilities will be evaluated when you return."

"Evaluated?" Circe said, shocked.

"Don't worry, it's nothing painful. It will be a quick test, so we can discover your powers and abilities and train you correctly. If you have filled out the rest of the form, you can explore the grounds and we will meet at the bandstand entrance in about half an hour."

Everyone finished their forms quickly and decided to look around. Alex rushed over to Circe and her dad.

"Might if I join you?" she asked.

"Not at all," Circe said, "It's hard to believe this place exists and no-one knows."

"Yeah, it is pretty amazing. So, do you have powers, or do you just want to be a hero?"

"Apparently I have powers…"

"Apparently? Don't you know?"

"Well, I once fired pinkish energy at some bullies and sent one through a window."

"Cool, and you haven't tried since?"

"Are you kidding me? Last thing I want to do is accidently hit someone or wreck something. I don't even know how it happened," Circe said, a bit shocked.

"Then, this place is definitely for you," Alex said with a smile.

"Yeah, hopefully I can get some answers. What about you?"

"Oh, I have a suit of armour, but it still has a couple of bugs in it."

"You're just saying that, so you don't have to show me."

"It wouldn't be impressive if I showed you and it didn't work."

"Are you sure we haven't met before? You look so familiar with the way your white hair covers your eye" Circe said, trying to place where she had seen Alex before.

"White hair? Circe, I have blonde hair, though not as nice as yours," Alex said, reacting shocked at first before quickly calming down.

"Ah thanks" Circe said, blushing, "Must be the light, as it looks like you have white hair."

"No, I'm a natural blonde" Alex said, relieved.

"Oh okay"

"We better start making our way back to the bandstand, or we might be left behind," David said.

"Okay Dad, I don't want to be stuck in some other plain of existence or whatever this is all week."

The trio arrived at the bandstand where Professor Fargo was already waiting with some of the other potential students.

"Ah Ms Goodwin, Ms Clúdach and Mr Goodwin, hope you enjoyed your brief visit?"

"Yes, Professor Fargo, it was enlightening," Circe said.

"That's good to hear and you Ms Clúdach?"

"It was interesting," Alex replied.

"Marvellous, so Mr Goodwin will you be allowing your daughter to attend Sunsport Super School?"

"It would give both of us some peace of mind, so as long as Circe wants to do it, I have no problems."

"Excellent, well it looks like we are all here, so let's head back" Professor Fargo said as he once more pressed his ring and almost immediately everyone was back in the park. Everyone left the bandstand.

"Before you all go, you will be getting a letter in the post which will reveal when we expect to see you again. Goodbye and stay safe."

"So, where do you live Alex? Maybe we can give you a lift home," Circe said.

"Thanks, but I live in Kingdom City" Alex said

"So how did you come down here, did you fly with your armour?" Circe joked.

"No, the flight system is something that I need fix, I took the train."

"Isn't the next train not until five?" David said.

"I believe so, so I have a couple of hours to kill."

"On your own? That's a bit unfair and a bit boring" Circe said.

"Well, I thought the whole hero thing would last longer, so I would have less time to kill," Alex said, scratching her head, trying to figure out what to do.

Circe looked at her dad, who quickly guessed what she was thinking and nodded in approval.

"Well, if you like I could help you kill the time," Circe sad with a smile

"I don't want to be a bother," Alex said.

"It's not bother, we didn't have plans anyway" Circe said.

"In that case, I would be delighted," Alex said.

"Great, I'll see you later Dad," Circe said, excited.

"If you need a lift, give me a ring and stay safe," David said.

"We will," Circe said.

"Don't worry Mr Goodwin, we're heroes in training" Alex jokingly replied.

The two girls headed out of the park and towards the City centre. As they did the two started talking

"Your dad seems nice" Alex said.

"He is, I don't know what I would do without him," Circe said.

"What's your mum like?" Alex asked not knowing.

"I don't have a mum?" Circe said shockingly to Alex not that upset.

"I'm sorry, I didn't know, I…" Alex said, getting flustered.

"It's okay, my Dad adopted me apparently when I was baby, and it has been just him and I since then" Circe said.

"Apparently?" Alex said, slightly confused.

"Well, my Dad hasn't told me the full story of my adoption, but he has promised me he will on my Birthday."

"That should be interesting, when's your birthday?"

"21st June."

"Lucky you, mine's Christmas Day and no, I don't get double presents," Alex said, a bit jealous.

"That sucks, so what are your parents like?" Circe asked.

"They can be strict, but they love me, even if they don't agree with some of my life choices."

"What do you mean?"

"Well, they are very traditional, and it isn't easy to change their minds."

"That must be hard."

"It can be, still I think we have arrived in the city centre" Alex said, trying to change the subject.

"You're right, so what do you want to do first?" Circe asked.

Almost on cue, Alex's stomach began to rumble.

"This is embarrassing," Alex said, blushing, "I was in a rush getting ready and trying to catch the train, I didn't get a chance to get some dinner."

"That's okay, I only had a light snack before coming, so where do you want to eat?"

"I don't know, what's your favourite place to eat?"

"Barring my dad's cooking, I love the Blaa Box."

"Never heard of it."

"It's a restaurant that specialises in filled Blaas."

"I don't think I've had a Blaa before," Alex said, trying to remember.

"Seriously?!" Circe said, shocked.

"I'm not from Sunsport remember? So, I never had the native dish."

"Oh right, maybe now is the perfect time to try one."

"It would be rude not to try the local cuisine, so let's try the Blaa Box."

"Great, it is this way," Circe said, taking Alex by the hand.

A short time later, Circe and Alex arrived at the Blaa Box, Alex was a bit confused she thought they were going to a restaurant not an old church surrounded by large walls. Circe quickly noticed Alex's perplexed expression.

"Is everything okay?" she asked.

"I thought you were taking me to a restaurant not a church" Alex said, still confused.

"This used to be a church but now it is one of Sunsport most popular restaurant," Circe explained.

"Never seen a restaurant with a graveyard before."

"You aren't scared of ghosts, are you?"

"No! It just so strange," Alex said as the two walked through the graveyard and into the Blaa Box.

Inside the old church, it was very busy despite being after lunchtime. The two young ladies headed to the counter to order. Alex allowed Circe to go first so she could have more time to study the menu. Circe didn't take too long to order, luckily by the time she had Alex had made up her mind. The two got a seat and waited for their food to come.

"So where in Sunsport do you live?" Alex asked.

"St. Declan's Castle, it's the castle on the hill across the river."

"You live in a castle, that's hard to believe," Alex said, not believing Circe.

"It's now a boarding school, but my dad and I have our own apartment in the castle since he's the janitor and cook."

"Ah, I see."

"What about you, where in Kingdom City do you live?"

"Em, I live near the train station. Just a regular house," Alex said, though Circe wondered why she hesitated but decided not to ask.

Very soon their food and drinks arrived. Alex was already impressed with what she saw in front of her.

"Wow, this looks great, what did you get?" She asked Circe.

"The Breakfast Blaa; sausage, rasher, black and white pudding and a hash brown, with mayo. What about you?"

"I went for the Christmas Blaa; Turkey, Sausage and Stuffing with mayo."

"So, breakfast for dinner and Christmas in Summer," Circe said, laughing.

"Why not," Alex said, also laughing.

The two eventually finished their meal and headed back towards the centre of the town. The two were having a great time, shopping, and talking. As they headed towards one of the city's shopping centres, Circe stopped in her tracks.

"What's wrong?" Alex asked noticing Circe stopping.

"See those people over there?" Circe said, pointing to the Puff Adders who were smoking outside of the shopping centre's entrances.

"Who? The people in the snakeskin tracksuits?" Alex said, looking at where Circe was pointing.

"Yeah, they're the Puff Adders."

"So?"

"Well, it was their leader that I sent through a window with my powers."

"Ah, I see."

"Yeah, and they see me!" Circe said, scared.

"Hey You!" Sam said angrily pointing at Circe as the Puff Adders rushed towards both ladies. Soon the group had surrounded both ladies.

"What do you want?" Alex said.

"Your girlfriend sent me through a window, and now it is payback time," Sam said angrily.

"Yeah right, are you trying to tell me someone like you, was thrown through a window by this little girl."

"Alex, don't antagonise them," Circe whispered.

"Too late for that," Sam said, punching Circe and knocking her over.

"Circe are you okay?!" Alex quickly rushed to help Circe up whose nose was bleeding.

"Aw, she's got a bloody nose," Kelly said laughing.

"You think this is funny?" Alex said angrily.

"Yeah! we do," Nicky said, punching Alex.

"If you knew who I was you wouldn't have done that" Alex thought to herself, before getting back up. She then hit her two bracelets together. Red and silver metal started to form around her and soon she was covered in her armour.

"What the hell?" Andy said, shocked.

"Who cares? It's the other Blonde we want" Sam said.

"Yeah, also that suit is just for show," Eddie said, laughing.

"Really?" Alex said with a smile though no-one could see it.

Alex's armour fired off a series of short energy blasts knocking all the Puff Anders over like bowling pins. With them on the ground for a moment, she quickly checked on Circe.

"Are you okay?"

"Yeah, I think my nose as stopped bleeding. This is your armour?"

"It is, though it is still buggy, I think those blasts are all it can muster."

"I don't think they were enough," Circe said, noticing the Puff Anders getting up and looking really mad.

"Oh no, apparently those blasts were too weak."

"That tears it, we are going to tear you out of that armour and give you both the beating of a lifetime," Sam said, seething with rage.

"Leave us alone!" Circe said as suddenly her hands began to glow with fuchsia energy.

"Circe?" Alex noticed the glowing hands.

Suddenly a massive fuchsia energy blast hit the Puff Adders sending them flying in all directions. Everyone nearby rushed to see what was going on, including two guardsmen.

Alex looked in amazement as Circe's hands were now covered in fuchsia smoke.

"What is going on here?" One of the guardsmen asked.

"These thugs attacked my friend and I, Guardsmen" Alex said, still wearing her armour.

"and who are you?" the other Guardsman asked.

"One second Guardsmen" Alex said as she hit her bracelets again, but nothing happened.

"Another error?! Are you kidding me?! Ah Circe can you give me a hand?"

"What's wrong?" Circe said, concerned.

"My armour won't retract, could you just…" Alex explained to Circe what to do and soon her armour retracted.

"Thanks, as I was saying Guardsmen, my friend and I were attacked by those thugs. We defended ourselves and those thugs ended up on the ground," Alex said.

"Are you two heroes?"

"Heroes in training, we just came from the Information day" Circe explained.

"I see, still we will have to ask you more questions at the station."

"But we did nothing wrong! It was those thugs over there" Alex said, pointing to the Puff Adders still on the ground.

"Still, we will have to confirm your story, for all we know you could be villains involved in a gang war."

"That's not fair" Circe said, beginning to cry.

"Let me handle this, you just stay here" Alex said, comforting her. "Guardsmen can I talk with you over there?"

"About what?"

"This." Alex showed them something which caused the Guardsmen to be shocked. About a minute later, Alex and the Guardsmen returned to Circe.

"Well Miss, your friend managed to convince us, of who you are, we are sorry for the way we acted, and we will arrest the offenders. Good day!" One of the Guardsmen said and the two then arrested the Puff Adders.

"What did you say to them?" Circe said, confused.

"Just the truth, now I still have time to kill, so do you still want to continue being my guide?"

"Sure, your armour was cool."

"It would have been better if it weren't full of bugs. Still your powers were impressive."

"If I knew how to control them."

"But in a way you do."

"What do you mean?"

"Circe you let off a massive energy blast and only those thugs were hurt, there wasn't even a dent on anything that should have been caught in the blast range."

"I really need to know more about them."

"At least your hands aren't smoking anymore."

"Yeah, they didn't take too long to stop the last time either. Still, I'm sorry you had to get involved."

"That's okay, we can look at it as Hero training."

The two continued going around Sunsport, until soon it was time for Alex to get the train.

"Thanks Circe, for being a guide, I had a really fun time."

"Apart from the run in with the Puff Anders. I'm sorry you got caught up in that."

"Like I said, it's okay. We got some practice and taught me that I have more bugs to fix."

"It wasn't a nice experience though."

"True, still I'll see you next week."

"Yeah"

"Cool. Looks like my train will be coming soon."

"Oh, do you have an email or a social media account, so we can keep in contact."

"My parents don't like me having one, but here's my mobile number and my email address."

"Great and here's mine," Circe said as the two exchanged numbers and email addresses.

Soon the two new friends waved each other goodbye, and Alex boarded her train. As Circe left the station, she decided to ring her dad.

"Hi Dad, I'm just leaving the train station."

"Okay, I'll see you in five minutes."

"I'll see you then," she said, ending the call.

As she walked up towards her home, she knew she had to tell her dad that she used her powers. Hopefully, he wouldn't be mad. She entered the castle and proceeded through the grandfather clock passageway to her home. She could go around the back of the castle to the back door, but this was always more fun.

"Dad I'm home!" She shouted.

"Welcome back," her dad said, "so how was your date?"

"DAD! It wasn't a date; I was helping someone around the city."

"Of course, you were" Her dad said sarcastically.

"I was, it wasn't a date, Alex is a friend."

"Then why are you blushing?"

"I'm…I'm not blushing I'm just warm from walking, that's all" Circe said, trying to defend herself.

"I'm messing with you, still was everything okay?"

Circe looked at her dad but didn't say anything.

"Circe, what happened?" her dad said, concerned.

"I used my powers," she said with a sigh.

"What happened?"

"Alex and I were heading towards the Siege Shopping Centre, when we were attacked by the Puff Anders."

"Are you okay? Did they hurt you?" her dad said, worried.

"They punched me giving me a bloody nose, but I'm okay. Alex tried to protect me with her armour, but it wasn't working properly. I was afraid and then my powers activated, and I blasted all five of them."

"At least you two weren't badly hurt," David said relieved.

Circe then explained what happened with the guardsmen.

"The sooner, we learn more about these powers the better," David said, "None of the parenting books I read had a chapter about superpowers."

"I'm sorry, Dad."

"Circe, you have no reason to apologise. Neither of us asked for this, but we will get through this," he said, hugging her.

"Still having a daughter who shoots energy blasts isn't what you were thinking of when you adopted me."

"Circe don't even think I regret adopting you. I would love you no matter what this means."

"Thanks Dad, that means a lot."

Soon, it was time to head back to the park and see what things will be revealed today. Hopefully, it would be answers, of course Circe was hoping to see Alex again. The two sat down on one of the benches surrounding the bandstand waiting for Professor Fargo to turn up. As they waited, Circe was already noticing some others from last week waiting. Soon a familiar face appeared.

"Hi Circe," Alex said, running over to her.

"Hi Alex, you look great," Circe said as the two hugged.

"Thanks, so do you. So, any more powers since last week?"

"Luckily no, hopefully I might get some answers. How's the armour working?"

"Still some bugs, but at least it opens on command properly."

"That's good, still no sign of your parents?"

"Nah, they are still too busy. At least your dad's here."

"Yeah, he's as anxious as I am to learn something about these powers?"

Soon, Professor Fargo appeared and led the group through the bandstand towards the hidden school. Inside he took the group to what looked like a waiting room.

"Thanks for coming, today I'll be testing your powers/abilities to better gauge how to continue your training. You'll be done one at a time and once you are done you can leave. I'll be calling you in no particular order."

Soon it was Circe's turn, Professor Fargo led both David and her into a large office. The office wasn't what they were expecting. It did have standard office furniture, but also a lot of books, strange artefacts and a lot of superhero, anime, and manga memorabilia.

"Okay Circe let's see;" Professor Fargo said, looking at a file; "apparently you can fire fuchsia-coloured energy blasts from your hands."

"That's right, professor" Circe said, slightly nervous.

"There's no need to be nervous, developing powers can be very frightening and our job here is to help people like you learn about them. So, you have no idea how your powers emerged."

"That's right, they just came out."

"Were you exposed to anything unusual at any time of your life?"

Circe looked at her dad, who was just as confused. "Not that I'm aware of."

"Circe hasn't been exposed to radioactive creatures or weird rocks or anything like that," David said, slightly annoyed.

"I'm just trying to figure out where her powers originate. I'm not doubting your parenting skills, Mr Goodwin. So, if they aren't artificial, they have to be natural."

"I don't understand," David said.

"Origins can happen in many ways, sometimes it is being exposed to a strange object, animal or chemical. It could be a magical artefact, or some technology bonded to a person. Sometimes it could be naturally occurring, something genetic passed out for a parent."

"I see…" David said, not really getting it.

"Circe, I would like you to hold this" Professor Fargo said, holding a dark orb, which then started to become yellow.

"What is it?" Circe said, slightly uneasy about touching it.

"Don't worry it won't bite. This orb responses to magical energies within someone and changes colour depending on the type of magic a person has and what they specialise in."

"You think Circe has magical powers?" David asked.

"Well, it is the easiest place to start, since I have magical powers myself, as you saw the orb went yellow, meaning I am an energy manipulator."

Circe still a bit hesitant took the orb from the Professor. The orb changed to white and started to glow. Professor Fargo looked in amazement.

"It's glowing white. What does that mean?" Circe asked amazed and confused.

"It…It means your powers come from a Divine source" the professor said, regaining his composure.

"What does that mean?" David said, concerned.

"It means that Circe's powers come from a God or Goddess. Either one of her parents is a deity and therefore she's a Demi-Goddess or a deity has decided to give Circe powers for some reason."

"This is madness, why would some random deity choose my daughter?" David said, unable to believe what was happening.

"Deities can work in mysterious ways," Professor Fargo said, "Circe, could you give your father the orb."

"Okay," Circe said, perplexed, David took the orb off his daughter and it went clear.

"It just went clear," David said, looking at the orb.

"Well, it means that you have no magical powers, so we can rule you out as being the source of Circe's powers. Circe, can you tell me more about your powers, the more information we have the better we can train you."

"Okay," she said with a deep breath, "As I mentioned in the form, I fire fuchsia coloured energy blasts. I have no idea how they work; they just seem to come out at certain times. The first time was when the Puff Adders attacked a clothes shop, Dad and I were in and I sent their leader through a window. The second time was when Alex and I were shopping, and we were attacked by the Puff Adders and I blasted all five of them. The strange thing was that even though the blast was big enough to hit all five of them, no-one and nothing else was it."

"Interesting, and how were you feeling before you fired?"

"I can't really say, I just wanted to stop them from hurting anyone," Circe said, trying to remember.

"Well, this does help a lot," Professor Fargo said, taking some notes.

"So, do you have any clue about my powers?"

"I have a better understanding, which will help me in researching your abilities. As far as I can tell, your powers have a divine source and so far, activate when you have a desire to protect someone or something. Also due to their mystically nature they will only harm what you want them to."

"That seems about right" Circe said.

"So, you think you can help Circe?" David asked.

"I do, of course I have to warn you, that it is possible that Circe may develop more powers as she progresses."

"More? We can barely get our heads around this whole energy blast power," David said, shocked.

"Don't worry Dad! We'll get through it."

"I hope so."

"Well, our time is nearly up as I still have other students to get through, is there anything else you want to ask before we wrap up."

"Actually, about other powers, since my powers first emerged and seem to be seeing things, even though people like my Dad can't. I even had my eyes tested and they were fine."

"I want to try something quick," Professor Fargo said as he quickly took something out of his deck and whispered what sounded like a spell. "Mr Goodwin, what do I have in my right hand."

"Nothing."

"Circe, what do you see?"

"It's a bit blurry but it looks like a stapler."

"It is a stapler," Professor Fargo said as the stapler appeared in his hand.

"How?" David asked shocked.

"I created a Fe-fiada, basically a barrier which makes things invisible. I helped create the one which surrounds the school, since people would still be able to see dimensional distortion. The fact that Circe has divine powers would allow her to see though the magic. The reason it seemed blurry is due to a lack of training, but that can easily be done."

"Well thank you, Professor Fargo, you have helped us understand her powers a bit," David said shaking the Professor's hand.

"No problem, hopefully our understanding will grow as Circe trains," Professor Fargo said, "Oh, and for you Circe, your training timetable and before you leave there will be a transporter device for you both which will allow you to come and go when you need to."

"Thank you, Professor Fargo," Circe said taking the sheet of paper.

Professor Fargo led them out of his office and called the next person, "Could Brendan Ross come into my office?"

A handsome man got up and walked past Circe giving her a smile. Circe smiled back. Soon Circe and her dad arrived where the transporters were been given out. The transporters came in various shapes. There were two staff members also at the desk.

"Hello, are you here for a transporter?" said, one of the staff.

"Of course, they are, why else would they be here?" the other staff member said.

"It's called being polite, bumhead."

Circe and her dad just looked at each other and waited for the two to stop arguing.

"Sorry about that, so you are here for a transporter?"

"Yes" said Circe, hoping they wouldn't start arguing again.

"Well, the transporters come in a variety of styles, you can either choose one of the items here or we can implant one into your watch or phone."

"Or we can do both," the other staff member chimed in

Both Circe and her dad opted for the phone implant. David also decided to get one for his watch, while Circe also took one of the transporter rings.

"So, you took one of the rings," David noticed.

"Well, I don't have much jewellery and it looked nice," Circe said, placing it on her finger.

"What's your training timetable like?"

"It looks like five half-day sessions, consisting of power training, hero protocol, self-defence, power theory and first aid."

"At least it is only half a day, and idea how long this training will go on for?" David asked.

"It doesn't seem to be that long, two months going by the dates, and I'm starting Monday week" Circe said, studying the timetable carefully.

"Do you need to get anything?"

"It says all I need to something to take notes with, so just some pencils, pens and paper. Everything else will be provided."

Father and daughter arrived at the bandstand and tried out their transporters, which worked without any problems. Now having some information, the two planned for Circe's training.

A week later and Circe was ready to start her hero training. The school year now over, so St Declan's Castle was very quiet and lonely as Circe and her dad walked through the great hall. Their footsteps echoed as they made their way to the front door. David made sure the doors were locked before getting into the car with his daughter.

"Soon, I'll be able to drive you into town," Circe smiled.

"How about we get you to learn about these powers before we get you learning to drive," David said, half worried about his daughter behind the wheel.

"I would be a great driver," Circe replied.

"I'm sure you would, but last thing we need is for you to accidently destroy the steering wheel."

"I'm not sure that's how they work but it's a good point."

With the schools finished until the autumn the traffic was quite light. As they headed towards the park, Circe decided to listen to the news headlines.

"Blast News! Hi, I'm Sarah-Jane. The Inclusive Relationship Bill is being made into law as of today. The Bill will legalise LGBT marriages and relationships for the first time and end the discrimination for many. Princess Edelgard, a prominent campaigner for the Bill said to Blast FM that the bill marked another step-in making Hibernia, a world leader in equality and a shining example for the world. In other news, The New Helvetica Museum was robbed last night; the guardsmen are still investigating what was stolen and hope to give an update later today."

"Robbing a museum, that's disgraceful," Circe said in disgust.

"Yeah, I hope they recover whatever was taken," David said, "a lot of those artefacts are irreplaceable."

Soon the small car arrived at the park. Circe carefully got out and headed towards the bandstand. When Alex also arrived and ran up behind her.

"So, ready for your first day of training," Alex said, excited.

"A bit nervous to be honest," Circe said.

"We'll be fine, what's your timetable like?"

Circe showed Alex her timetable.

"Hey, it is the same as mine," Alex said, looking at her own timetable.

"At least that means we will be in the same class," Circe said happily.

"True, going from last time, there weren't many people especially if you remove the parents," Alex said, thinking back, "By the way; did you hear the Inclusive Relationship Bill is being passed."

"Yeah, there will probably be celebrations all over the country when it is passed. Shame I couldn't vote for it."

"Same here."

"The Princess couldn't even vote, and she was one of the main people behind the campaign."

"Yeah, and her dad won't even allow the voting age to be reduced," Alex said as if she took it personally.

"Still, it got passed, which is the main thing," Circe said.

"Yeah, well we have arrived, so who wants to do the honours?" Alex said as they arrived at the bandstand.

"I'll do it," Circe said, activating her transporter ring.

The two arrived outside the school, where were a couple of more people around, probably instructors. The two headed inside for their first day.

Chapter 3
Infodumps and Toy Variants

The two ladies headed into the lecture hall, where their first class will be held. While they were a bit early, there were already some other people in talking. The ladies took two seats as some of the other heroes in training noticed.

"Check out the two that just walked in, Brendan" One of the boys said.

"Forget it Dermot, they're probably both gay," Brendan said.

"Don't say that, still we should introduce ourselves," Dermot said.

"You just want to chat them up."

"Quiet! They might hear you," Dermot said, trying to make Brendan lower his voice.

However, before the two could talk to Circe and Alex, some more people entered along with Professor Fargo.

"Okay everyone, take a seat and we can start your training," Professor Fargo said

Circe and Alex had a quick look around. There were eight people ready to begin their training including them. Both ladies were interested to see what types of powers they had. Then Professor Fargo began to speak.

"Welcome everyone, you have all met me, but you haven't met each other. So, this is an introduction day, it would be best for everyone to introduce themselves. Don't worry it isn't going to be much, just stand in front of your peers and tell them, your name, where you are from and your powers. But please tell your powers, don't show. Last thing we need is people getting hurt or property being damaged."

"My name is Circe Goodwin and I'm from Sunsport City. I can fire Fuchsia coloured energy blast from my hands, and I can see invisible objects."

"I'm Alex Clúdach and I'm from Kingdom City. I have an armour that has numerous features like energy projection, advanced scanners and flight."

"I'm Brendan Ross and I'm from New Helvetica. I have super strength and can fire energy beams from my eyes."

"I'm Dermot McGrath from Mammoth Fort. I can grow twelve feet tall and gain super strength."

"I'm Siobhán Regan from Hexford. I can control the weather (barely)"

"I'm Declan Walsh from Sunsport. I have super speed."

"I am Aoife McCarthy from Crimson Cove and I can generate bright light."

"I am Patrick Deasy from Piketown, and I can generate electricity."

"Thank you all, a good range of abilities and with proper training, you will all be able to master your abilities and become heroes. Of course, some of you are probably more used to your abilities than others, but you may learn new skills or tricks that you never thought of before," Professor Fargo said. "Well let's go through the classes."

"Power Training is where you will learn to train and improve your powers. Hero protocol is where you learn about the rules and regulations about being a hero, sadly it is a theory class, so it can be quite boring. Self-Defence is where you will learn to defend yourself without using your powers. Power Theory deals with different powers and abilities you may encounter, while First Aid will deal with saving lives. These classes will be taught by myself and other heroes, you will be meet as your journey begins. So, any questions?"

Everyone shook their heads.

"Excellent, now I give you a tour of the area, and then I suggest you get to know each other better."

After the tour, the young heroes all meet up outside, to learn more about each other's powers.

"Hopefully, we won't break anything," Dermot said.

"Professor Fargo said it was okay to use our powers here, so I doubt we will," Siobhán said.

"So, who wants to go first?" Alex asked.

"I'll go first," Brendan said. He picked up a huge rock and throw it into the sky, he then fired a blast of red energy from his eyes, which destroyed the rock. Everyone clapped their hands.

"Thank you! Thank You! So, who's next?" Brendan said, taking a bow.

Dermot stepped up, he began to grow until he was the size of a giant and then began to juggle two large rocks.

"Maybe with some training, I can grow bigger and stronger," he said as he put down the rocks, to a round of applause.

Siobhán went next.

"Just to let you know, I haven't mastered my powers yet," she said nervously.

"That's what we are all here for, so don't worry about it," Alex said.

She began to say a spell, suddenly the sunny sky turned dark as clouds formed and then hailstones and lightning started to appear.

"I only wanted a little cloud!" Siobhán shouted as everyone ran inside. Thankfully Siobhán's spell didn't last long.

"Sorry about that," she said meekly as the sun returned.

"Don't worry about it, we all make mistakes and there's no way any of us have mastered our abilities," Circe said.

"Yeah, at least that didn't last long," said Patrick.

With the skies clear again, the power showcase continued. Alex decided to go next. She banged her bracelets together and her armour formed around her. She showed of some of her armour's features but decided against flying just in case she crashed. When she was finished, she deactivated her armour to another round of applause.

"Thank You! Thank You!" She said.

"Did you really build that armour yourself?" Aoife asked.

"Yeah, but it's still a work in progress, the flight mechanism is off and thankfully I think I have fixed the armour deactivation system.

"So, no more getting stuck in your armour," Circe said with a smile.

"Hopefully, that's the case" Alex said, "So, who's next?"

"I'll do it," Aoife said.

Aoife rubbed her hands, and activated her power, suddenly there was a bright light, which forced everyone to close their eyes.

"Ah, I forgot, I can't really show off my power without blinding everyone."

"It was still quite a display, well what we could see of it," Declan said as everyone began to open their eyes again and clapped.

Patrick rubbed his eyes and decided to go next.

"Hopefully, I don't shock anyone," he said, causing everyone to take a couple of steps back.

He let rip with an amazing lightning display, luckily none of the blast hit anyone, though there were a couple of near misses. Still, it was impressive, leading to another round of applause.

"Glad everyone is safe," Patrick said, wiping his forehead.

"First time, I haven't been first for something," Declan said, ready to go.

Declan quickly ran around the area, each time trying to go faster, with everyone timing him. Soon he stopped running but wasn't out of breath.

"Shame we couldn't see what speed, I was doing," he spoke.

"About 81km," said Alex.

"Did your armour tell you that?" Declan asked.

"No, just some simple maths," Alex replied with a smile.

"That just leaves Circe," Brendan said, looking at her.

"I can't," she said nervously.

"Come on, firing energy blasts can't be that bad," Brendan said.

"Hey, don't pressure her," Dermot said.

"It just that I don't know who they work. They only activated a couple of weeks ago and I so far haven't figured out how to fire them on command."

"So how do they work?" Siobhán asked.

"According to Professor Fargo, so far they seem to be reactive. Apparently, I need to want to protect someone or something in order for them to activate.

"That's a shame."

"Well, I'm hopefully I will understand them better while I'm here. Sorry I couldn't actually show you them."

"It is a shame, those blasts are really powerful and pretty," Alex said.

"You've seen her powers?" Brendan asked.

"Yeah, she saved my life, I think my armour recorded some of it," Alex said, checking her armour's files. Soon she found the footage and thanks to a hologram projector everyone got to see Circe's powers in action.

"You floored five thugs at once!" Brendan said, shocked.

"Are they dead?" Patrick asked.

"NO!" Circe said, shocked at the question.

"Sorry!" Patrick apologised for his question.

"Miraculously only the thugs were hurt, nothing else was damaged," Alex said, explaining more on what she saw.

"Are we all enjoying showing off our abilities?" Professor Fargo asked checking on his students.

"Yes Professor!" All the students replied.

"How did you know what we were doing?" Aoife asked.

"A lot of your powers aren't very subtle, shall we say. Still, I think we can call it a good introduction day, so I'll let you go home now, and we'll see you back here tomorrow for some Power Training. Class dismissed!"

The students headed to the transporter and warped back to the park. They parted ways except for Circe and Alex who started walking together.

"So, what are you doing now?" Circe asked.

"Heading to get a train."

"Isn't it going to be expensive going up and down on the train every day?"

"Luckily, my parents are paying for it."

"Still, it would be expensive for them."

"True, but they are happy to help me. They are very supportive on most things."

"So, are you planning to join in in the Inclusive Relationship Bill celebrations?"

"Yeah, I'm taking part in the Kingdom City celebrations."

"That will be massive, maybe you'll see the royal family."

"I'm pretty certain I will."

"That must be amazing."

"It's okay," Alex said, almost dismissing it.

"If my dad allows it, I might head into town to see what's happening."

The two young ladies eventually parted ways at the train station and Circe headed home.

"Dad, I'm home!"

"Welcome back, how was your first day?" David said, hugging his daughter.

"It was just an introduction day. Though I did feel a bit left out."

"Oh?"

"Well, after we all introduced ourselves, we decided to go outside, and everyone started showing off their powers. They were throwing boulders, making it rain and other amazing powers, but I couldn't show mine," she said, sounding a bit upset.

"Hey, Hey, it's okay. You'll get control of your powers. After all, that's why you are going to this school," David said, comforting her daughter.

"Thanks Dad," she said, feeling better.

"Also, next week will be your birthday."

"Yeah, though it looks I'll be having lessons that day," Circe said, checking her timetable.

"We will still celebrate it, don't worry about."

"And you will still tell me about my adoption?"

"I'll tell you everything, in fact you are having lessons that day will give me time to get some things."

"What things?"

"You'll see on your birthday."

"Also, I was wondering, would it be okay if I go into town later to check out the celebrations. Please?"

"I know that bill was important to you, so okay. Just be very careful and be back before ten."

"I will, thanks Dad," she said, hugging him.

Shortly afterwards Circe arrived in the city centre, where already there was a crowd gathering. Circe meet up with her friends and told them about her new training and powers.

"So, who knew you had superpowers," Fiona said, surprised.

"I didn't," Circe said.

"Still, it must be exciting "Yu said, excited.

"Not really, I'm firing energy blasts that I can't control, and I can see invisible objects as well. To be honest it is scary," Circe said.

Don't worry, you'll probably be a natural at it," Claire said, trying to cheer Circe up.

"I don't know about that."

"Hey, I think the royal family are about to appear," Fiona said.

Everyone looked at the large screen that had been installed in the centre so everyone could watch the royal family. King Brian along with his wife Sarah and their daughter Edelgard appeared to the huge crowd in Kingdom City. The Princess was wearing a blue dress with gold accents. Her white hair which covered her left eye was tied up into a bun with a silver tiara on her head.

"I love Princess Edelgard's dress;" Fiona said.

"She looks amazing" Claire said.

"And strangely familiar," Circe thought to herself.

On the screen, King Brian gave her daughter a microphone. With a deep breathe she addressed the people.

"I am going to keep this 'speech' brief. This is a momentous day for Hibernia where people are allowed to love each other without any barriers or prejudice. While I could not vote myself, I want to thank everyone who could and did for making this all possible. I also have to thank my father and this land's government for allowing this to happen. For everyone who this law affects; this is your day!"

The princess handed the microphone back to her father and took another deep breath as crowds all over the country cheered.

"At least it was short and sweet," Fiona said.

"Yeah, still this is a big day, and we know she hates doing speeches" Circe said, excited with the whole event.

The friends continued to enjoy themselves before heading home as not to get into trouble with their parents.

The next day, Circe, Alex and the other students arrived for Power Training. They were only again welcomed by Professor Fargo.

"Welcome back, students! Today is Power Training. In this class you will learn how to control your powers and safely use them. As well as myself, you will have other teachers to help you since you have different powers."

The students looked in amazement as their other teachers arrived. Elemental, Hyperdrive, PainTrain and Hex Queen all entered the room.

"As well as helping you with your powers, these are your other teachers. Elemental and Hyperdrive teach Hero Protocol, PainTrain teach Self Defence, and Hex Queen teaches First Aid while I teach Power Theory as well as acting as your mentor. Now that the introductions are out of the way, let's get started. Circe will be training with me, Elemental will be training Patrick and Declan, Hyperdrive will be training Alex. Brendan and Dermot will be trained by PainTrain, while Hex Queen will be training Siobhán and Aoife. Before we start, each student will be asked to change into specially designed training wear."

The students looked perplexed, but Professor Fargo directed them to dressing rooms where training outfits consisting of t-shirt and tracksuit trousers was waiting for each of them. To all their surprises, they fitted perfectly.

"How did they know our sizes?" Circe asked concerned.

"I think the material used, automatically shapes to our bodies," Alex said, admiring the fit.

All the students emerged from the dressing rooms and soon everyone broke off into their training groups and went to separate areas as to make sure they didn't get in each other's way.

"Okay Circe, let's try to fire off a blast," Professor Fargo said

"But I don't know how," Circe said, not even knowing where to start.

"Well, that's what this class is for. Think back to the previous times your powers emerged, what happened?" Professor Fargo said, reassuring her.

Circe thought for a minute before answering, "The first time the Puff Adders were going to destroy a shop and hurt my Dad and the shopkeeper. The second time, they were going to hurt Alex."

"So, the common factors are a group of delinquents and people in danger. Well since I'm not going to allow some thugs on campus, we will have to go with your desire to help or protect someone. Think about someone you care about and you want to protect and imagine firing a blast."

Circe took a deep breath and tried to imagine someone she cared about in danger. It was a horrible thought and despite her best efforts nothing happened.

"I'm sorry Professor Fargo, but I can't do it. I'm a useless hero," she said, upset.

"Nonsense. You have just started your journey. I never expected you or anyone to be masters of their powers in one class. Let's try something a bit different," Professor Fargo said, comforting her and thinking about something else to try. "So far your powers are reactive…"

Circe still didn't feel good, everyone else could use their abilities at will while she couldn't. Suddenly Professor Fargo swung his cane at her. Suddenly Circe's hand glowed and she fired a blast of Fuchsia energy at the professor, sending him flying across the training area. Everyone looked shocked as Circe ran after the Professor.

"Oh my God, Professor! I'm so sorry!" She said, panicking.

"Don't be my dear. This isn't the first time I've been sent flying by someone, and I doubt it will be the last," he said, dusting himself off. "Also, I should be apologising for doing that to you. I probably frightened you."

"A bit," Circe said, relieved she didn't badly hurt him.

"Okay people, nothing to see here," Professor Fargo said, making sure not to cause a fuss.

"But Professor!" Elemental said, concerned.

"I'm fine Elizabeth."

"If you say so."

"Well, that was educational," Professor Fargo said as Circe helped him up.

"I'm not sure firing my Professor across an area is educational."

"Don't be so pessimistic. Thanks to that, ahem, demonstration, I learned that you acted instinctively, so subconsciously you do know how your powers work. Also, despite flying across the room, your blast didn't do any damage, which means that you weren't trying to kill me or maybe you can't kill with your powers. So, let's try again."

"You aren't going to try and hit me, again, are you?" Circe asked worried.

"No, let's try it without the need for violence."

"But we tried that."

"But now we know some more things. Since it is mystical in nature and the way it acts, let's try some simple spellcasting techniques. Imagine a small light at your fingertips."

"Okay…"

"Relax, I have taught many students this technique. Now once you see that light, try focusing more energy into it, make the light brighter and bigger."

"I'm trying, I can see the light, but I can't make it bigger."

"Don't force it, seeing the light is a good start. Whenever you are ready try launching the light, imagine flicking it or sending it off like a rocket."

Circe's hands began to glow, and she looked with excitement as she seemed to finally be able to fire a blast on her own. Then a small ball of Fuchsia energy just flopped from her fingertips on the floor. She looked at Professor Fargo who looked back at her and the two of them just laughed.

"That was anticlimactic," Professor Fargo said, laughing.

"I was hoping for something more spectacular, but it just flopped literally," Circe said, trying to stop laughing.

Eventually the two stopped, before the others wondered what was going on.

"Well, it's a start," Professor Fargo said.

"Still, it could have gone better."

"Stop being so hard on yourself. You couldn't even fire a shot before today. Of course, a good experiment is only as good if the results can be repeated so try firing another shot."

Circe tried again and once again her arms glowed and a slightly larger ball of energy flopped from her hands.

"At least we know the first one wasn't a fluke and that you can use your powers at will," Professor Fargo said with great encouragement.

"Well, I couldn't have done it without your help," Circe said, smiling.

Eventually class end for the day. The students met up to talk about their first taste of hero training.

"Ouch, PainTrain is an appropriate codename" said Brennan rubbing his shoulders.

"Yeah, and we are going to have him for self-defence as well?" Dermot said, not looking forward to more sessions with PainTrain.

"Hex Queen was surprisingly very nice," Siobhán said.

"Yeah, she was. You see her in action, and she seems really scary, but she's a lovely person once you get to know her," Aoife said, agreeing with Siobhán.

"Elemental was a fun teacher," Patrick said.

"Yeah, with a nice bum," Declan said.

"Pervert!" Aoife shouted.

"Yeah, she's a married woman," Siobhán said with disgust.

"And you two don't look at married guys," Declan said.

The two ladies made some barely audible noises.

"Speaking of her husband, Hyperdrive gave me some ideas of improving my armour," Alex said, excited with thinking about the new ideas she had.

"Professor Fargo was a huge help," Circe said.

"Is that why you shot him across the room?" Brendan asked with a smirk.

"I didn't mean to!" Circe said, horrified.

"So, can you control your powers?" Alex asked.

"A bit."

"Come on show us," Brennan said.

"It's not going to be very impressive," Circe said.

"Oh, stop making excuses and show us," Alex said, really happy Circe could control her powers.

"Okay, Okay" Circe said. She took a deep breath and remembered what she was taught. Soon her hands began to glow in now a familiar fuchsia light. Everyone stepped back to give her some room and make sure they wouldn't go flying like the Professor did. Once again, another energy ball just flopped onto the ground.

"Not as impressive as the one you used against those thugs, but hey you can control it," Alex said, happy and supportive of Circe.

"I was hoping for something better," Brendan said, which got him some angry looks from the ladies. "Em, it was still great for your first try," he said quickly.

"Don't worry about it," Siobhán said, "We are all still learning, when my abilities emerged, I could barely summon a cloud.

"Yeah, I was barely able to light up my hand at first and now look at me," Aoife said

"Except we couldn't look at you, you were too bright, remember" Patrick said, pointing out Aoife's blinding demonstration earlier.

"Circe knows what I mean."

"Hey, we should all go and celebrate Circe learning about her powers and surviving out first day of hero training," Dermot said, excited.

They all agreed to that plan and soon headed towards the city centre to have some fun and to get to know each other better.

Eventually the class of budding heroes headed home. Circe arrived home where her father welcomed her.

"So, how was your first proper day?" He asked excited.

"It was interesting, I am starting to get some control over my powers," she said.

"That's great!"

"I also accidently fired my teacher into a wall," She said, almost under her breath.

"Circe!" He shouted.

"It was an accident. He was trying to get my powers to activate, and they did and shot him across the room" Circe explained.

"Did you hurt him?"

"I said he was fine, and I think somehow my powers didn't actually hurt him, not like the other times they went off."

"So, show me what you learned," her father said, excited.

"It's not going to be impressive, just to warn you."

"Still, I want to see."

"The two headed outside where Circe couldn't do any damage to their home, though so far her energy blasts hadn't destroyed any property. Still, it was better to be safe than sorry.

"Is recoding this really necessary?" She asked noticed her dad recording her with his phone.

"I have recorded all of your firsts, and this will be no exception."

She wasn't sure about being recorded but if it made her dad happy, she wasn't going to argue. As before she charged her powers, and her hands began to glow. Her father watched in anticipation and as before a small ball of energy just fell out. She looked at her dad, who looked backed at her and he started to laugh.

"Hey, you are supposed to be supporting me, not laughing at me;" she said as she started laughing herself.

"I'm sorry sweetie, it's just that the way your hands were glowing, I was expecting something like you did to that thug.

"So far, that's all I can do."

"Maybe you can stop villains by making them laugh."

"That's not funny."

The two calmed down and went back inside.

"Sorry, it wasn't that impressive for your recording," Circe said.

"Maybe not, but it was still important and no matter what, I am proud of you."

"Do I dare ask how many embarrassing recordings you have of me?"

"Embarrassing? None. Precious? Loads" He said with a clear smile of pride.

The first week had already reached the halfway point. Today's class was Hero Protocol with husband-and-wife team; Hyperdrive and Elemental. The students took their seats as the two heroes entered the room.

"Good morning young heroes," Elemental said, "and welcome to Hero Protocol. Terry and I will be teaching you everything you need to know about operating as a hero and what the public and government will be expecting of you as heroes. To be honest, this is a theory heavy subject, but we will do our best to have fun."

"Yeah, no-one wants to just sit here and listen to me go on and on. 'Lizzie' on the other hand, I could listen to all day and not be bored," Hyperdrive said.

"You will be hearing a lot of my husband sending a lot of flattery my way. I apologise in advance for all of it. Just try to ignore anything he says that isn't relevant," Elemental said, apologising for her husband's behaviour.

"Before we starting going in all the theory, we thought it would be a good idea for us to have a Q and A session. If you have any questions about heroes and heroics, ask away and we'll try out best to answer them. Hyperdrive said.

The young heroes thought for a minute, and Alex was the first to ask.

"Should heroes have secret identities? Like, in the past it was common but these days there are very few if any heroes who seem to have any?"

"Secret identities are a bad idea," Elizabeth said, "Their effectiveness has diminished over time given that cameras are now practically everywhere. Image editing software means that Domino masks and the like can easily be digitally erased, and the resulting images can be plastered all over the internet. Then there is the added stress of trying to keep it secret from your friends and family and what that does to your normal life. Also, there is no point thinking that keeping your identity secret is going to keep your loved ones safe, as a villain could just easily target them even at random; in fact, they seem to do it even without knowing."

"I see," Alex said, clearly having some something to consider.

"Do we have to become heroes after we complete this course?" Circe asked.

"Ah no," Hyperdrive decided to answer this question. "This is only a brief course designed to help you to learn the basics of heroics. This course will also give you some legal protection if something were to happen with your powers. There are more advanced courses for people who want to be heroes. While we do get a number of people who just want to control their powers and live a normal life; we have noticed that once you get the hero bug, you might not stop. Still, we do stress, no-one is forcing you to wear a costume and fight crime."

"Thank you," Circe said, slightly relieved.

"Will we get getting costumes?" Aoife asked.

"That will be up to you," Elemental said, "However we do suggest something, in fact we will be talking about costumes and codenames after this Q and A. Including what is and isn't appropriate."

"Cool," Aoife said, excited.

The Q and A eventually ended, and the two heroes began to talk about costumes and codenames, with Elemental doing most of the talking.

"Your costume and codename are important when you become a hero." She started to explain, "Your costume should reflex you and if you want your powers. It should aid not hinder your powers and/or abilities; so, if you had something like superspeed you wouldn't want to have a costume that would slow you down. Very importantly you want your costume to be comfortable; especially as you could be wearing it for long periods of time."

"What about capes?" Patrick asked.

"Capes are a tricky subject. They have been around since heroics began and can really improve the look of a costume. Of course, we all know the dangers of capes like revolving doors and the like. However, if you want to have a cape, there are some opinions like a shorter cape or have a method that the cape can detach if enough force is applied."

"How did you come up with your costumes?" asked Siobhán.

"Well, I designed mine to be comfortable and it represent myself." Elemental explained, "It has a skirt and boots because that's what I love to wear and what I feel most comfortable in. The leggings are there to prevent any unwanted panty shots. Which anyone considering a dress or skirt as part of your costume, should consider. The colours reflect my two-tone hair, just I went for gold and black instead of ash-blonde and black."

"And you look amazing in it, and anything else you wear," Hyperdrive said.

"Terry," Elemental said, about to blush, "Maybe you should explain your armour instead of trying to embarrass your wife."

"I'm just telling the truth. Anyway, my armour was designed in order to allow me to fight along my wife."

"Something I was against by the way."

"Still, my armour is designed for speed, while trying not to compromise on protection. That meant making it out of a material that was lightweight but extremely durable. When it came to weapons, I decided to use an energy sword and shield as that was what I had training in. Of course, I added the expected stuff like flight and scanners. The key part of my armour was making sure it was able to protect itself and its

71

user when it goes into Hyperdrive mode. After that, the rest of the colours and design cues were personal choice."

"What about your codenames?" Dermot asked.

"That was easy," Elemental said, "I got mine from my mum when she decided to retire."

"While I decided to call myself and my ability, Hyperdrive because it sounded cool," Hyperdrive said.

"So, now you have some insight into costume design and codenames, we would like you to start thinking about your own possible costumes and codenames. We would like to see some ideas for our next class," Elemental said.

"Seriously, homework?" Brendan said, shocked.

"This is a school, and we aren't asking for a finished product just some ideas and maybe a rough sketch. Elizabeth said. "With that class dismissed."

"This sucks. Getting homework, I thought we were learning to be heroes," Brendan said, clearly annoyed.

"Come On, it isn't that bad and besides, it is important for us to get a start on this," Aoife said, clearly excited.

"What if we aren't good at drawing?" Dermot said.

"I don't think it matters, Elemental said even a rough sketch would do," Circe said, reassuring.

"Yeah, they're heroes not art critics," Alex said.

That evening Circe began to work on her costume, she already knew what colour it was going to be, but she was trying to think of a design. She had her sketchbook and pencils but so far, her rough sketches didn't seem to scream superhero.

"So, have you decided on your super suit yet?" Her dad knocked as he entered.

"Nah, I haven't decided on a design yet."

"But you have decided on the colour" Her dad said, noticing all the costumes were Fuchsia.

"It is my favourite colour."

"Athrú," Circe heard a female voice whispering.

"Did you hear that?" Circe asked her dad.

"Athrú" the female voice whispering again.

"Hear what?" Her dad asked confused.

"A female voice whispering."

"Circe, you are the only lady here, unless you invited someone over."

"Athrú" the female voice whispering again.

"I haven't and seriously you can't hear someone whispering."

"No, maybe this is another power, like the way you can see invisible things. What are you hearing?"

"Athrú," the female voice whispering again.

"I'm hearing a woman say 'Athrú'!"

A flash of light happened. Circe looked, as bands of fuchsia energy wrapped around her body. As they did, her clothes seems to change to resemble a costume, complete with gloves, boots, leggings, and a split piece of fabric. The costume had some Celtic markings, and her eyes were now fuchsia as well.

"Circe?" her dad stared unable to believe what just happened.

"Dad?" she said, nervous and shocked.

"What on Earth happened?" They both shouted.

"I don't know, just kept hearing a woman whispering 'Athrú'."

By saying the word again, Circe's clothes return to normal, leaving father and daughter still confused.

"Looks like I'm back to normal and thankfully whatever happened didn't destroy my clothes," Circe said, relieved and looking at her normal clothes.

"Still, what happened?"

"I don't know, it must be part of my powers, I should really talk to Professor Fargo about this."

"That would be a good idea but wait until morning. At least you don't have to worry about trying to think of designs for your costume."

"That's true, shame I didn't actually get a good look at it before I transformed backed," Circe said. She could try transforming again but decided to wait and tell Professor Fargo about it first.

"You mean this," her dad had somehow managed to record the whole transformation.

"How?" Circe was dumbfounded.

"As I said, I record all of your firsts, so I'm always prepared," he said proudly as he handed his daughter his phone. She quickly looked at the recording.

"Do you think it would be okay, if I used one of the school's printers to print off an image?" She asked.

"Just don't go overboard. It is due to the school's generosity that we are allowed to use any of the school's facilities."

"I know and I'll be careful," Circe said as she headed towards the school.

She grabbed a torch as she headed out, there was no need to start lighting up all the school's lights especially for one person. Also, it was Summer, so the school halls were still lit by the light of the evening sun. For some, going around an empty castle turned school would be scary but for Circe it was her home so there was never anything to be scared of.

She reached one of school's computer labs and transferred the video to the computer and slowly scanned the video for a good capture of the costume. As well as been a great cook, her dad was also great with a camera. Soon she had the image she wanted and transferred the video and image to her phone. She printed out the image and deleted her work. Once she had gotten what she had wanted, she headed back.

For the rest of the evening, Circe's mind was racing with questions as she studied the video and the image. Who or what was that voice that only she could hear? Was it linked to her powers? Was it linked to her adoption? Was there any meaning to the designs on the costume? She tried her best to clear her head of all these and many more questions, as she eventually headed to bed. Tomorrow was another day and hopefully Professor Fargo might help her.

Another new day meant another new class, this time it was self-defence with PainTrain, a class that after what Dermot and Brendan had told them all about PainTrain, no-one was really looking forward to. They all put on their training outfits and headed to the training area where PainTrain was already waiting for them. A mountain of man wearing train themed armour, he was not someone you wanted to get into a fight with.

"Right, I'm here to teach you all self-defence. You can't protect people, if you can't protect yourselves and you can't rely on your powers all the time," PainTrain explained in a serious tone. "So, with that explained, we will be sparing one-on-one. Each of you will try your best to either subdue me or at least try and get me to step out of this circle and remember you can't use your powers."

The young heroes all looked at each other, even if they could use their powers, it was unlikely to help them. This seemed more like an exercise in futility.

"Okay, ladies first, so we will start with Aoife," PainTrain said, looking at his list of students.

"Gulp," went Aoife she was terrified, and it wasn't long before her fears were confirmed. The 'fight' had barely begun, and she was on the floor.

"Okay, next we'll have Circe try," PainTrain said as Aoife pulled herself up.

Circe nervously stepped into the Circle. She could just control her powers and even then, a little energy ball wasn't going to stop PainTrain. Also, how was she supposed to subdue him? She couldn't think of anything when PainTrain gave the order to start. She barely managed to avoid his first punch, when suddenly her hands began to glow. Before, PainTrain could react, she blasted him right across the room.

"Goodwin! You aren't supposed to use your powers!" PainTrain bellowed.

"I'm sorry! I have very little control over them, and they react when I'm threated," Circe said, apologising.

"Bloody mystics," PainTrain said annoyed under his breath. He went over to a bag he had near one of the walls and took out two metal bracelets, which still mumbling. "Here put these on."

Circe was confused, but not wanting to get into trouble put on the bracelets.

"What are these?" She said, looking at them.

"Iron bracelets, with those on, you shouldn't be able to use your magic. Iron negates mystical energies, especially if they are Faerie or Divine in nature."

She wasn't sure about that, but still it was worth not getting into trouble. So, she and PainTrain started again, and this time PainTrain sent her flying.

"Ow!" she said as she got up.

"Not so easy when you can't blast things, is it?" PainTrain said as he removed the bracelets.

"No, sir," she said, still sore.

"That's two teachers you shot across the room," Alex said with a smile.

"It's not something to be proud of," Circe said as she sat down on the bench with the others.

"Okay, since you think Circe's little performance was so cool, you're next, Alex," PainTrain said, still annoyed that Circe blasted him across the room.

"Sir, yes Sir," Alex said, with a sound of confidence in her voice.

The two took their positions inside the circle. As they began, Alex took a strange fighting stance, which had everyone confused. As PainTrain launched his attack, Alex managed to grab his wrist with incredible grip and slowly managed to flip the teacher out of the circle. Everyone was shocked but quickly started to cheer.

"Where do you learn that?" Circe asked the question that was on everyone's mind.

"From watching various TV shows," Alex said it was clearly a lie, but at this point no-one cared.

"Okay, that was well done," PainTrain said, "but I have to remind you all, that there are still five people left, so don't start the celebrations yet."

Sure enough, the next five fights ended with PainTrain easily defeating his students. They all sat on the bench while PainTrain addressed them.

"So, do any of you know my we had this exercise?"

"Because you love to attack kids?" Brendan said, which quickly got him a death glare from PainTrain.

"No, it was to test your ability to defend yourselves first-hand, and as I suspected you are basically civilians, except for one, Ms Clúdach."

"It was just a fluke," Alex said, realising what she had done.

"I doubt it, still now I know what all of your skill levels are, I know how to teach you. Still, you are all probably sore from today's class. So, rest up and we'll being proper training next time."

After changing, the class decided to head off. However, Circe planned to stay behind.

"You coming Circe?" Alex asked.

"No, I want to talk to Professor Fargo about something," she replied.

"Is everything okay?" Alex asked concerned.

"I'm not sure, last night I... magically summoned a costume," Circe said, trying best to explain what happened.

"Oh, you have to show me."

"I want to talk to Professor Fargo about this. I'm sure clothes appearing from nowhere is not normal. I want to be sure there is nothing dangerous about it."

"Then you'll show me?"

"Okay, if it is safe, I'll show you, but are you sure you want to wait around, I don't know how long I'll be."

"It's fine."

With that Circe headed towards Professor Fargo's office. However, as she arrived at the door, it was clear he was in a meeting with someone. Inside Professor Fargo and Hex Queen were talking to the Guardsmen about the robbery at the New Helvetica museum.

"Was this all that was taken?" Professor Fargo looked a photos of the object that were taken.

"That's correct. According to the museum the item in question is the Blade of Balor. While it is valuable, there were more valuable artifacts in the museum," one of the Guardsmen said.

"So, clearly it was specifically targeted," Hex Queen said.

"That's correct. We were hoping that as two of the region's best magic users, you might have an idea on why it was stolen."

"It is clearly a ceremonial blade, but details on the Blade are very sketchy," Hex Queen said.

"That's true, but the design of the blade clearly points to what type of ceremony," Professor Fargo said.

"And what would that be Professor?" One of the Guardsmen

"It's used to raise the dead," Professor Fargo said dead seriously.

"Necromancy? Are you sure?" Hex Queen was shocked.

"I'm sure, Vivian."

"But why this artifact in particular?" Hex Queen was confused.

"That's why we asked for your assistance. We were hoping that you would know," said one of the Guardsmen.

"We will do everything we can to help and uncover why it was taken and hopefully retrieve the Blade," Professor Fargo said

"Hopefully, this is just some theft and wouldn't end up like the Rathdaggan incident with that breaded idiot."

"Let's hope so, but let's not forget Necromancy can be very dangerous, no matter who uses it," Professor Fargo said dead seriously.

The two Guardsmen thanked the two teachers and left passing Circe as they did. Circe wondering what was going on, but it was probably none of her business. She knocked on Professor Fargo's door and entered inside.

"Oh, I'm sorry, I didn't know you were in a meeting still," Circe said, seeing Hex Queen.

"It's okay," Professor Fargo said, "Is something the matter?"

"Well, there has been a new development with my powers."

"Good thing, you have two magical users then," Professor Fargo said, reassuring her, "So, what happened?"

"It would be better if I show you," Circe said, "Athrú!"

Just like magic, she changed in front of the two teachers. It was strange but surprisingly fun.

"A Magical Girl transformation!" Professor Fargo said, excited.

Circe had no idea what he was on about, but it seemed to have lifted his mood from whatever the meeting was about.

"Interesting, most magic users would be lucky to be able to change their clothes like that. Mine just change with a snap of my fingers nothing that flashy," Hex Queen said.

"What's a Magical Girl transformation?" Circe had to ask.

"Oh sorry. It's when a person with powers has an elaborate sequence to changing from civilian to hero. They are more common in other parts of the world, but it can happen anywhere. The fact that you have one, might help explain why you have little control of your powers. When it comes to Magical Girls, their powers mostly can only be used when transformed."

"What is also interesting is your 'command' word or whatever they call it. Athrú is Gaelic for 'change' or 'transform' and some of the symbols on your costume do suggest a Gaelic origin."

"So, this is a good thing?" Circe had to ask, since the two teachers weren't making much sense.

"This is a very good thing," Professor Fargo said, "It will help a lot when it comes to learning and controlling your powers."

"That's a relief," Circe said, delighted, "Athrú!"

By saying it a second time, her costume vanished, and her regular clothes reappeared.

"Thank you two so much," she said as she headed off to meet Alex.

"When did she have her awakening?" Hex Queen was now curious about Circe.

"Roughly two maybe three weeks ago," Professor Fargo said, "Why?"

"A girl with Divine class magic with possible Gaelic origins, gets her awakening a few weeks before an ancient item named after the Fomorian King is stolen…" Hex Queen was thinking out loud.

"You aren't suggesting Circe has something to do with the robbery?" Professor Fargo was shocked.

"No, but the timing it very close. I'm thinking that Ms Goodwin's awakening happened due to what was going to happen…"

Unaware of what her teachers were discussing, Circe had met up with Alex.

"So, everything okay?" Alex asked.

Circe quickly caught Alex up to speed with what the teachers had told her.

"Well, what are you waiting for, show me?" Alex said, excited to see Circe's costume and transformation.

"Okay, Athrú!"

Alex looked in amazement as Circe clothes transformed. For Circe, this was starting to become second nature.

"Wow! Talk about a transformation!" Alex said, checking out Circe's outfit.

"Eh, Thanks. I think I'm getting used to it now," Circe said.

"So, does it do anything?"

"I don't know, to be honest I would prefer to wait until we have training again before experimenting," Circe said, clearly being cautious.

"Makes sense, still mind if I take some scans with my armour, to see what it is made off," Alex asked.

"You can try, though with this being magical, I'm not sure if your armour will be able to scan it."

"Hey, it's worth a try," Alex said as she hit her two bracelets together and her armour formed around her.

"Hey, you sort of have your own magical girl transformation.!" Circe said with a smile.

"More like a metallic girl transformation and I think your transformation is flashier. Now let's see what we have."

Alex began to make as detailed scan of Circe as she could.

"So, did your underwear magically transform or is it just your clothes," Alex asked jokingly.

"I don't know. I haven't even tried to take it off, and don't start scanning my underwear!" Circe said defensively.

"Relax, I wasn't going to. I'm not a pervert, not sure about some of the lads in the class though."

"You know, it's hard to know if you are joking or not when you are wearing the helmet."

"I know, but I can't scan you without it. Okay I'm nearly done, any idea why your eyes change colour?"

"No Idea, but since I can see invisible objects maybe it helps me see them clearer?" Circe was just guessing little knowing she was correct.

Well, I have finished the scan, so you can transform back if you wish," Alex said, quite pleased with the results as Circe transformed back. "Aww, your reverse-transformation isn't as flashy."

"I think because it is a magical girl transformation and not an ordinary girl transformation."

"True, still from what my armour could gather and remember I'm not a magic expert, it seems your costume is at least knife and bullet proof, so it does offer some protection, there are other readings I don't really understand, but I can email you the results and you or Professor Fargo can look over them."

"That would be a big help, thanks," Circe said, delighted as Alex's armour retracted.

"No problem," Alex said, "So, what are your plans for your birthday?"

"Don't really have much of the way of plans. Apart from present and cake, the main thing will be learning about my adoption. I'll probably meet up with some of my friends from school as well."

"So, what are you getting, or do you know?"

"Oh, I getting a really cute Fuchsia party dress, I was lucky to find it, especially as it was exactly my budget."

"Budget?" Alex said, a bit confused.

"Yeah, my dad's job isn't exactly a high paid job. Don't get me wrong, he enjoys his work, and he does everything to support me, still he does have to budget everything, that includes presents."

"I see, so if someone was to get you something…"

"It would have to be less than €50 and much less, otherwise it would probably hurt my dad's feelings. He even has to remind my grandparents not to go over the budget. Still, I don't expect you to get anything."

"Why not, we're friends and I want to get you something."

"Just don't go overboard."

After hanging out for a bit, the two friends parted ways. Alex needed to think of a gift for Circe and send her the results of her scans. Circe headed home to tell her dad about what she had learned about her magical girl transformation.

"So, at least the costume change is a good thing," her dad said, relieved that his daughter was okay. "and it allows you to control your powers power better?"

"That's what Professor Fargo and Hex Queen said, though I'm not sure until I train with Professor Fargo again."

"So, no Superhero Circe?" Her dad said, slightly disappointed.

"Sorry Dad, but last thing I want to do is accidently shoot our home."

"I understand, when you are training with Professor Fargo again?"

"Next Tuesday."

"Which is your birthday."

"Yeah. It is going to be strange to be learning on my birthday. Most years I've been lucky and avoid it."

"You are going to have a good time no matter what."

"I know I will, Dad."

The two hugged and enjoyed the rest of the day, which including trying to figure out the results of the scans Alex did. However, that night Circe found it very hard to sleep. She was plagued with nightmares. She woke up with a massive fright and a scream. Her dad rushed in.

"Circe! Are you alright?"

"It was terrifying. There was this giant cyclops, and he was shooting eye beams and the whole city was on fire. There was death and chaos, and people were getting really sick, and it was all so real," she said, clearly scared and upset as her dad wiped away her tears.

"It's okay, it was just a bad dream," he said, doing his best to comfort her.

"It was just so real."

"Some nightmares can be like that. Just try to get some sleep."

David kept an eye on her, until she did fall asleep. Though he wasn't sure if he was going to be able to sleep. He was hoping it was just a nightmare but with Circe's developing powers, it was hard to tell.

The morning sun vanquished the horrible night; and soon Circe and David were heading towards the school.

"How did you sleep afterwards?" David asked, noticing Circe didn't look her usual self.

"I managed to get some sleep, still that nightmare was terrifying," Circe said, trying to forget the nightmare as she turned on the radio to catch the news.

"Blast News! Hi, I'm Ciara. Guardsmen have released new information on the robbery of the New Helvetica Museum, which happened a few nights ago. Guardsmen are looking for anyone who as any information about the theft of the Blade of Balor. The incident is believed to have happened around 3.32 a.m. and anyone with who noticed anything suspicious in or around the museum is asked to contact their local Guardsmen Station. Superintendent Jones released a statement warning that the criminals involved will be caught and are continuing their investigation."

"The Blade of Balor, the name sounds familiar…" Circe said, thinking.

"I'm sure we saw it on one of your many trips to the museum," Her dad said.

"It's not just that, the name Balor sounds familiar."

"It will probably come to you in time, just focus on learning and leave the detective work to the Guardsmen."

"But, if I become a hero, I might have to solve crimes like this."

"You have a point, but you are still learning, so focus on that."

"Don't worry, I will."

The Goodwins parted company and Circe was greeted by her fellow classmates.

"Morning guys!" She said.

"Man, Circe you look terrible," Brendan said, which quickly resulted in a dig in the ribs by Dermot.

"You idiot, you should always compliment a lady on her looks," he whispered angrily.

"Sorry, I didn't sleep well last night," Circe said, yawning.

"Everything okay?" Alex asked.

"Just had a really bad nightmare," Circe replied.

"Well, hopefully today wouldn't be too bad," Aoife said, trying to pick Circe's spirit's up.

"I hope so."

Luckily, it was First aid with Hex Queen. Hex Queen was a very good teacher, using her magic to help visualise what she was teaching. It was a surreal experience, but it helped Circe focus on the class and not on her bad night. With the class over, their first week of hero training was over. The small class decided to get some dinner together to celebrate.

Afterwards, she arrived home, her dad was off getting some groceries, so she had the whole school to herself, which wasn't something new but still strange. She headed to her room, with the name Balor again nagging her. She decided to check some of her books, many she had since she was a child. She loved reading and drawing, so many of her presents over the years were books. She wondered where to start and was about to pick one of her books, when suddenly…

"Not, that one! The one on the right."

It was that voice again. The same one that told her how to transform. She looked around her room and even looked around the apartment. Nothing.

"Who's there?" she shouted. No reply.

She looked at the book, the voice told her to pick. It was her book of Irish myths and legends. Sure enough, there was Balor of the Poisonous Eye, the Formorian God and King who was a giant who killed anything just by looking at it. This shocked Circe as the drawing resembled the creature from her nightmare. Why was she having nightmares about some mythical God and what did it have to do with her and what happened at the museum. Just when one thing about her new powers was starting to make sense, something else would then come and put her back at the start. Her dad soon returned, and she explained what had happened, with the voice and the image of Balor.

"Just more things to work out," he said, hugging her. "Just try focusing on the positives so far. You have gone from randomly shouting energy blasts, to having a little control and getting a costume in last than a week."

Her dad was right, she had managed to do so much in such little time and in time hopefully she will get more answers. Also, it was the weekend, so it would be better to put thoughts of ghosts and giants away and enjoy the weekend. With that, Circe's weekend was quite quiet, thankfully no more nightmares or ghostly voices. Soon a new week began.

Today's class was Power Theory with Professor Fargo. While it was as the name suggested mostly a theory class; Circe didn't mind as it would help her understand more about the superpowered world she had now entered. She arrived at the park and noticed there was a lot more people around. As she transported to the school, it also seemed that there was a lot more people around as well, some in costumes, others just wearing regular clothes. After manoeuvring through the more crowded hallways, Circe arrived at the classroom where Siobhán, Dermot, Aoife and Patrick had already arrived.

"Did you see the amount of people around?" Siobhan asked.

"See it? I just went through it," Circe said as she took her seat.

"They could have warned us. How come there is so many?" Patrick said.

"Last week must have been like a Freshers' Week, you know, where only the newbies come in, so they can get use to the place without having to worry and be overwhelmed," Dermot said.

Soon Alex, Declan and Brendan arrived.

"It's nuts out there," Alex said, "I was tempted to try and fly through the window."

"Is that even allowed?" Circe asked.

"You could try, but the windows don't open from the outside, so either someone would have to let Ms Clúdach in, or she would have to force the window open herself, which would be a very bad idea," Professor Fargo said, entering the room.

"Okay class, welcome to Power Theory. This class will focus on the different types of powers out there. Also, you probably all noticed the increase of both students and teachers around the campus. Well, naturally as not to overwhelm you, you were given a freshers' week to help you all settle.

Hopefully, the influx won't affect your experience here too much."

"Now given my own experience, we will start by looking at magic. Magic comes in four main types. The first is Divine, which is when a person is bestowed powers by a God or Goddess. This can be done by a Divine entity either being the parent of the person in question, making them a Demigod or Demigoddess. It can also be done by a Divine entity blessing a person with powers, either by the person finding favour with the Divine Entity or the Divine Entity could be bestowing the powers as a test or some kind of joke."

Circe paused from taking her notes when she heard that. It was bad enough she was trying to learn these powers, the idea that some all-powerful entity could be having a laugh at her, and her dad's expense was frightening. Still, she tried to get that horrible notion out of her head and focus on the class.

"When using an Omen Orb to detect magical powers, the orb will glow white to indicate a person has Divine powers. Power-wise, the person could have anything, it may have something to do with the Divine Entity that their powers come from or it could be something different. It is also for this reason and the fact that Divine powers aren't common among the magical community that information on Divine powers is sketchy and usually requires one on one training and development."

"Was the Omen Orb, the orb you used when you tested me and I'm assuming everyone?" Aoife asked.

"It was and yes, everyone here was tested with it. Since Hibernia is a land of magic and the supernatural, it makes sense to have the Omen Orb as standard testing procedure."

"Can the Orb be wrong?" Circe asked.

"It can be fooled, but that requires vast knowledge and power to do so. Other than that, it is always accurate."

"Do we have any Gods among us?" Brendan asked.

"That is personal information, and it is up to any individual to reveal their origin, be it magical, mutation or something else."

"Ah okay."

"Anyways the second magical type is Energy Manipulation. This is probably the most common type of magic in Hibernia and for many the easiest. Energy Manipulation is when a magic user channels and manipulates the energy either internally or from external sources. For most, the results are simple energy blasts but for more powerful and experienced they can alter the energy around them, for example a person who can manipulate electricity on a basic level could fire lightning, but a more experienced user could manipulate the electricity in appliances or even manipulate the electrical impulses of the human body."

"That's a frightening thought," Dermot said, shocked.

"Indeed, that's why while we train you in the use of your abilities and try to help you reach your potential; we also expect you to use them responsibly. Of course, there is no light or dark side to energy, just how they are used. While manipulating the electrical impulses of the human body would be considered evil, it could be used by a hero to subdue a dangerous criminal. When using an Omen Orb to detect magical powers, the orb will glow yellow to indicate a person has Energy Manipulation powers."

"Now, Natural Magic has similar properties to Energy Manipulation but focuses on manipulating the natural world. When using an Omen Orb to detect magical powers, the orb will glow green to indicate a person has Natural powers. This can be anything from manipulating the natural elements of wind, fire, air, and earth; it could be weather manipulation or manipulating plants or animals."

As with all forms of magic the more experienced; the more powerful and creative the user can be. For example, a person who can manipulate the air might be able to just create a gust of wind, while a more experienced one could manipulate the wind around them or even fly. Natural Magic is also very difficult to master, especially as it does require bending the natural world but not breaking the rules of the natural world. You couldn't for example making it snow on a summer's day unless the temperature was also lowered. For many Natural Magic users, they will focus on one part of their powerset and develop that. Next, we will look at some videos of these types of magic in action."

"Professor Fargo, you said there were four main magic types, but you have only mentioned three," Circe said, looking at her notes.

"So, I have;" he said, looking at his own notes. "The final type of magic is Necromancy."

"Isn't that forbidden?" Alex asked.

"Indeed, it is. Necromancy is a forbidden and dark form of magic, which manipulates the dead. This can range from controlling zombies to fully raising the dead. This does require a lot of power and skill to use, also most necromancers require a magical artifact to either perform the spells necessary or control the dead. As it breaks all-natural law and ethics, Necromancy is forbidden in Hibernia and most of the world. When using an Omen Orb to detect magical powers, the orb will turn black to indicate a person is a necromancer."

"If it is forbidden, is it okay to for you to be teaching about it?" Siobhán asked a bit worried.

"I am only teaching you about it, I'm not teaching you it. There is a big difference," Professor Fargo assured her. "Beside this has to be covered as part of the hero curriculum, so no-one here is going to go to jail."

That's a relief," Patrick said.

"Now, if there are no more questions, let's watch some videos of the various types of magic being used."

The rest of the class was a lot of fun video watching, which ended early, so the young heroes in training decided to hang out.

"So, what's everyone's origin?" Brendan asked.

"Didn't Professor Fargo tell you that where our powers come from is supposed to be personal," Alex said.

"Says the girl who doesn't have powers. Still, it would be a better way for us all to get to know each other. Who knows some of us might have similar origins, like being caught in one of those mass-empowering events. Also, Professor Fargo said it is up to the individual if they want to reveal their origin," Brendan said.

"Okay, how about we put it to a vote? How many people would be happy to explain their origin?" Dermot said, trying to prevent an argument starting.

Everyone thought about it, before everyone barring Alex (who had no powers); Circe and Patrick, put up their hands. For them all, Circe wasn't a surprise given she seemed to only recently got her powers. Patrick though was a surprise.

"Looks like a majority," Brendan said.

"Yeah, but if you two don't want to tell us your origins that's fine," Dermot said, "For me, I got my powers from my parents. My dad can grow, and my mum is super strong; so, I have a genetic quirk."

"I fell into a barrel of toxic waste and instead of dying; got powers," Brendan said.

"That was lucky," said Aoife. "Anyway, I have a mutant genetic quirk, as my powers aren't linked to my parents."

"I accidently overloaded a treadmill which supercharged my body," Declan said, slightly embarrassed.

"I'm a Natural magic user, specialising in Weather Manipulation," Siobhán said.

"Well, that's everyone," Dermot said, "Unless you two have changed your minds. If you haven't that's fine."

"I'm just afraid you'll think different of me, if I did reveal it," Circe said, she felt bad not being able to show them her powers when the others did, so she didn't want to be left out again.

"No-one will, we are all friends, right?" Alex said as the others nodded. "Still, like we said, you do have to if you don't want to."

"Thanks, it's okay," she said, taking a deep breath. "I have Divine magical powers."

"Really?" Brendan said, interested.

"No way, you're a God?" Aoife said, shocked and excited.

"I don't know. All I know is that when I did the Omen Orb test it said I had Divine powers. That's it," Circe said.

"Well, you have the looks of a Goddess," Alex said under her breath.

"Did you say something Alex?" Siobhan asked.

"Ah No."

"So, you don't want us bowing to you or offering you a sacrifice?" Aoife said, joking.

"No! Like Professor Fargo said, it could be some Divine being giving me powers for some reason," Circe said.

"Still, I'm glad you shared it with us," Brendan said.

"Well, I might as well tell you," Patrick said, not wanting to be left out.

"You don't have to," Circe said.

"It's okay, I got my powers from... licking a battery during a lightning storm while camping," Patrick said, clearly embarrassed.

"There's nothing to be embarrassed about," Siobhán said, "There are worse origins."

"Yeah, like that guy who got hit by a cursed rubber duck," Aoife said.

"Still thanks for being so understanding guys," Patrick said.

"No problem," Circe said with a smile.

After sharing their origins and learning more about each other. Circe headed home to tell her Dad, about what she had learned about Divine powers. The two pondered about where her powers came from, with the new information she had gotten.

"I still don't see why some being would give you powers," her dad said as they both looked over Circe's notes.

"Professor Fargo did mention it could be someone playing a cruel joke. You know, let's give a random girl superpowers and have a good laugh about it," Circe said, it was still a thought she hated but it could be a possibility.

"It's not a joke," the mysterious female voice appeared once again, causing Circe to look around.

"What's wrong?" her dad asked.

"It's that woman's voice again. Are you sure this place isn't haunted? Or am I going insane?"

"As far as I know, there are no ghosts here and you are definitely not going crazy," he said, trying to reassure her.

"But you don't hear her?"

"No, I don't. What's the voice saying now?"

"Apparently my powers aren't a joke."

"Well, that's good news."

"If you believe the ghost woman."

"This is the same voice that led to your costume appearing, and that Balor creature, so for the moment the voice seems friendly and is trying to help."

"Let's hope it stays that way."

The talk about power theories and ghost voices went on for a bit longer. However soon the day gave way to night and after that the Summer Solstice had arrived. Which for Circe meant one thing, her birthday. She quickly got up, showered, and got dressed before heading to the small kitchen where her dad was already making breakfast.

"Happy Birthday Circe!" he said, kissing and hugging her.

"Thanks dad," she replied with a smile.

She sat down as her father handed her, her breakfast. As the two enjoyed it, Circe was already thinking about what her day was going to be like. It was then that her dad handed her a paper bag.

"I hope you like it," he said.

Inside the bag was an envelope along with her new dress. She opened the envelope to reveal a birthday card with a generic superheroine and the words' To my Super daughter!' on it. Circe could only smile at the thought and joke. She then read the inside of the card and gave her dad a huge hug. She then took out the dress and marvelled at it.

"Oh, I really want to wear it," she said.

"That's for special occasions," her dad reminded her.

"What could be more special, then the birth of your only daughter?" she said with a smile.

"You know what I mean."

"I know, but it's so pretty."

As a compromise, she put on the dress, so she could get a couple of photos to show her friends. With that, the two headed to the park. The news was talking about there were still no leads on the theft of the Blade of Balor, as well as some political stuff. As the two parted company, Circe headed to the bandstand where Aoife and Siobhán had also just arrived.

"Morning Circe!" Aoife said.

"Morning guys, great day!"

"Yeah!" Siobhan said, enjoying the sunny weather.

"Perfect weather for the Summer Solstice and someone's birthday!" Alex said, having just arrived.

"Who's birthday?" Aoife asked.

"Mine," said Circe.

"Aw, you should have told us, we could have gotten you something," Siobhán said, feeling a bit bad for not knowing.

"It's okay, in fact, it is strange to be going to school on my birthday."

"Still, we have to do something," Aoife said.

"Well, I'm going to meet some of my friends from school, after we are done, you are all more that welcome to come along," Circe said.

"Sure, sounds like fun," Alex said, excited.

The four girls headed to the school as Circe filled them in on her other friends. As it was Power Training, they and the boys who had also arrived, headed to the training area, where the teachers were already waiting.

"Welcome to your second week of Power Training," Professor Fargo said, "Today, your tutors will continue to expand on what you did last week, so be prepared. Before we start, we have to wish Circe a very Happy Birthday."

Circe was a bit embarrassed but appreciated it. Soon, the heroes and heroes in training once again divided into their respective groups. Professor Fargo and Circe took their positions.

"So, have you been practicing?" Professor Fargo asked.

"As best as I could," Circe said.

She showed off what she had learned. Her hands glowed in a now familiar glow and a small energy ball flew from her hands, it didn't go far but it didn't just fall the ground like it did last week.

"Getting better," Professor Fargo said, impressed with the progress. "Okay please Transform into your costume."

"Okay, Athrú!" She said, causing her costume to appear.

This caused the others to stop, as barring Alex, they hadn't seen her magical transformation. Brendan was quite taken by the transformation and the resulting outfit, which got him blindsided by PainTrain.

"Get your head in the game, Ross! You shouldn't be distracted especially by another hero changing," he said, not apologising for the cheap attack.

"Ouch, yes sir," Brendan said, rubbing his head.

While Brendan was still recovering, Circe and Professor Fargo were still practicing.

"Okay, try firing an energy blast now that you are 'powered up'," he said.

Circe once again powered up a blast, this time it fired off perfectly. With some encouragement she fired off another blast and another. Somehow using her powers was a lot easier in her costume. She didn't need as much time to charge up a blast, in fact they seemed to come almost instantly.

"I don't get it," she said, looking at her slightly smoking hands.

"When it comes to your powers, what we are seeing is your natural state. Given the nature of your powers, if you are a demigoddess, then this would be your goddess side, where you are easily access your powers. So far, we have been trying to access your powers from your mortal side, which would explain the difficulty," Professor Fargo explained.

"Speaking of my powers, there are some things I want to talk about."

Circe explained about the female voice she was hearing, along with the nightmare she had about Balor.

"The voice must be from someone who gave you your powers, probably trying to help you learn about your powers. The nightmare about Balor could just be your mind being influence by the news reports, or it could be a prophetic dream," Professor Fargo said, thinking out loud.

"So, I could possibly be seeing the future?"

"Or at least a possible future, as nothing is set in stone, though if you ever dream about lotto numbers make sure to remember them. Still there is something I would like to try, especially as you are powered up. I'm going to make my cane invisible using a Fe-fiada and then I'm going to swing it. I want you to try and stop it. Don't worry I wouldn't actually hit you with it."

"Okay…" Circe was a bit hesitant, especially as last time he swung his cane at her, he ended up across the room.

The two got ready and Professor Fargo swung his cane. Not only could Circe see it, but there was a strange fuchsia outline of him as well but slightly ahead of where he actually was and seemed to be moving downwards. Seeing the outline movements, she moved her hand to block the downward swing. To both of their surprise, she managed to stop it.

"Impressive, how did you know I was going to go low?"

Circe explained what she had saw.

"Well, we now know that your ability to see invisible objects and the like is improved by your transformation. It also seems you have some precognitive abilities, as you could see my moves."

"It was a bit disorienting."

"I'm sure it was, seeing two of someone, but you did very well for your first try. Still, I want you to keep practicing, even when you aren't in costume."

After some more training, class for the day ended. Circe and the other girls headed into the city, to meet, Claire, Fiona and Yu. With the introductions out of the way, the ladies all began to go to a restaurant to eat. Aoife and Siobhán still felt guilty that they didn't have a gift, despite not knowing until this morning. So, before everyone handed Circe her gifts, they made an excuse to go to the toilet. After a while, which had the others starting to worry; they returned with shopping bags.

Now that they are all been reunited and all clearly having gifts, they could all now give Circe her gifts. Fiona gave her a new purse, Yu gave her a load of art supplies, Claire gave her a model car, since she was now seventeen; Aoife gave her a dog plushie, while Siobhán gave her a scarf. Alex gave her a beautiful necklace.

"They are all beautiful, thank you so much; seriously you guys didn't have to go to all this trouble for me," Circe said, really touched.

"Think nothing of it, what are friends for," Fiona said.

Circe then showed them images of her new dress and they all went shopping. Eventually they all headed their separate ways, with Circe bring all of her presents home. While she would love to walk, she wasn't going to be able to carry everything, so it was decided to take the bus. Usually, her dad would pick her up, but she knew he was preparing to finally tell her where she came from and he had said he needed to get some things. Her dad had been putting off this talk for years and now it was happening she was having mixed feelings, she wanted to know but what if the details were too horrifying. How would it affect her dad or their relationship? She entered the castle and opened the door behind the clock which led to her home. She arrived at the door at the end of the corridor and took a deep breath as she turned her key and opened the door.

"Dad! I'm home!" she shouted.

"Hi honey!" Her dad said, delighted and gave her hug. "So how was your day?"

"Busy, people shouldn't have to go to school on their birthday."

"Well, sadly that can happen. So, are you ready to learn how I adopted you?"

"Ready as I'll ever be," Circe said with a deep breath.

"Okay, come into the sitting room."

The two entered the sitting room, where on the table there was a small basket with a Celtic Triskelion on it, a book, some blankets and a small piece of paper. Circe was surprised and confused, she had never seen any of these items and she wondered what they all meant. She looked confused as she and her dad sat down.

"What are these?" she asked confused.

"Everything, barring a couple of nappies, that was with you when I found you," her dad said.

"Found me?" She said, shocked, "I don't understand…"

"You will, it was a dark and stormy night."

Circe just looked at her dad, for using such a terrible cliché.

"It was… anyway, it was around three thirty-two in the morning when I heard the castle doorbell ring. I went straight to the door, hoping that it didn't wake anyone else. I opened the door to find a baby crying on the step."

"What?" Circe said, shocked.

"I found you on the step outside the front door in this basket," her dad said with a deep sigh as he handed his daughter the basket.

"I was in this?" Circe said, looking at the small basket.

"You were, wrapped in these blankets. I brought out of the storm and tried to calm you down. The doorbell and your crying had woken the deacon, who wondered what was going on. We took you into this very room to get you warm. Luckily, it didn't take much to calm you down. I checked your basket for any clues but the only things in it were a couple of nappies, along with a book and a note."

"Wait, I was abandoned…" Circe said with tears starting to form.

"I sorry, but you were," he said, comforting her and wiping away her tears. "Do you want me to continue?"

"Please do."

"Okay, as I was saying, the only other things in the basket, were this book and this note."

"Osborn's book of Greek Myths?" Circe said, reading the cover, "Why was this with me?"

"Read the note."

"Choose a name from this book and keep her safe" Circe said, confused about the note.

"That was it. Seeing you looking at me and the way you smiled at me, made me want to keep you. I talked about it with the deacon and my parents, and after a couple of days, I legally adopted you as my daughter. Coming up with a name was tricky but I read through the book a couple of times, and I liked the name Circe, also since I found you and were probably born on that day, I was inspired by the Celtic pattern on the basket to give you the middle name of Summer, since 21st June is the Summer Solstice."

"So that's why you named me Circe, I was always puzzled on why you called me that. Still, it doesn't explain why whoever abandoned me here would want me named after someone from Greek Mythology."

"I have no idea, I didn't get it myself, but I decided to honour that wish."

"Do you have any idea who abandoned me?"

"I'm sorry Circe, I have no idea. You were the only person around when I found you. I even checked the school's security cameras, and I couldn't see anyone. It was almost like you were magically placed on the doorstep."

"Maybe whoever left me on those steps used a Fe-fiada, like Professor Fargo used. Maybe they did it, so no-one would know who it was."

"Circe, do you want to find your real parents?" David said with a heavy sigh. He didn't want to ask the question, but Circe had a right to know. "Whatever you decide, I'll support your decision."

Circe looked at her dad, with tears starting to swell and gave her dad a huge hug.

"Thank you! Thank you so much!" She said in a stream of tears.

"I don't understand."

"You took me in after I was abandoned, you raised me as if I were your own daughter even though you didn't have to. Thank you, Dad!"

"It was nothing Circe. If I had to do it again I would. You are the greatest thing that happened to me," he said with a smile as he wiped away her tears.

"Dad, I don't want to find my biological parents. You are my dad; you are my real parent. Whoever gave birth to me is some stranger who abandoned me on a doorstep, they clearly didn't care for me or want me."

"If that's the way you feel, then that's fine."

"You sure?"

"It's your decision, if you don't want to know then you don't have to."

"Thanks Dad!" Circe said, giving her dad a huge hug.

"So, how about some birthday cake?"

"Yes, please I can't wait to see what it is."

Her dad quickly brought in a homemade banoffee birthday cake; Circe's favourite; sang happy birthday and after she had blown out the candles; both of them enjoyed a slice.

"This is delicious," she said, enjoying every bite.

"I'm glad you like it," her dad said proudly.

Afterwards, Circe showed her dad the gifts her friends had given her. They then watched a popular program that her dad had watched when he was a child with aliens that had made a comeback. Circe was surprised to see her name listed on the birthday rollcall but knew that it would also mean something to her dad, and it was a nice surprise. Eventually the two headed to bed. Circe had a great day and was glad she now knew where she came from... Well to a point. There were still questions about her birth and abandonment, which were clearly linked to her powers, but for now she wasn't interested in finding out. She knew who she was and that was what mattered. As she fell asleep, she didn't hear the female voice wishing her a happy birthday.

Chapter 4
A Baptism of Fire Will Leave You with a Burnt Forehead

The weeks passed and the young heroes in training were getting more confident with their powers and roles. Meanwhile an ancient evil was about to strike Sunsport. It was a calm night, and two young people were walking around the city after meeting in a local pub.

"Thank you for a good time," said the man.

"No problem, you seemed a bit lonely, and I thought you might like some company," said the woman. She had beautiful white porcelain skin, ravishing red lips and fantastic fair hair.

"Still, there were plenty of other guys you probably could have gone with."

"Are you not glad, I chose you?"

"Oh I am."

"That's great, let's go this way." The woman said, taking the man by the hand and leading him into a side street.

"Okay, where are we going?"

The young woman began kissing the young man all over. He didn't mind and started doing likewise. As they did, the lady's features changed revealing fangs and monstrous eyes. She quickly plunged her fangs into the man's neck draining him of his blood and life.

"One less man, to ruin this world," she said as she reverted to her human appearance.

The dead man's body was left on the street and was eventually discovered by another couple. Soon the Guardsmen were called along with Professor Fargo. While some of Guardsmen talked to the couple who had discovered the body, Professor Fargo examined the body with some Guardsmen. After examining the body with some mystical objects. Professor Fargo stated his findings.

"Well, you were right, it is the Dearg Due," he said with a sigh.

"The Red Blood Sucker! That foul villainess vampire," said one of the Guardsmen annoyed.

"At least now with the heroes we can finally catch her." Another Guardsman proclaimed.

"Unfortunately, it isn't that simple. Most of the heroes and even our students are off on various missions," Professor Fargo said.

"But this could be our best chance to finally stop her. She is very cunning, but she will probably need to feed again."

"I know, but the only regular heroes are a class of trainees. They haven't even completed any exams yet," Professor Fargo said.

"Rookies are not, we will need all the help we can get, especially super powered help."

"I'm taking you are making this an official request for assistance."

"Sadly, I am."

"Very well, I'll inform the students tomorrow."

The next day Circe and her fellow heroes in training got a surprise message from Professor Fargo, they were told to meet him in one of the school's conference rooms. As they entered the room, Professor Fargo was there waiting for them. There was a large round table with a projector in the centre. As they all took a seat, Professor Fargo began to talk.

"I'm sure you are all confused about this, but I'll explain. The Guardsmen have asked for assistance and due to other heroes' and students' other commitments, you will be assisting them."

"Wait, but we are still training. Can they do that?" Circe asked surprised.

"Unfortunately, they can. If the Guardsmen make an official request, then legally any and all heroes that they make that request to, have to assist; unless there are extreme circumstances," Alex said.

"Very good. I see someone has been brushing up on the law," Professor Fargo said.

"Eh, yeah, can't enforce it if we don't know about it," Alex said, sounding strangely nervous.

"This is who you will be assisting the Guardsmen in stopping. Her name is the Dearg Due" Professor Fargo said as a holographic image of the Dearg Due appeared on the table.

"She's hot," said Dermot which made all the ladies stare at him. "What? We're all thinking it."

"I've heard about her," Circe said, "According to legend, she was a woman who everyone wanted to marry but was in love with a peasant. Her father forced her to marry a chieftain, so he could become rich. The chieftain didn't even love her, he just saw her as a glorified trophy and he would beat her just to take pleasure of seeing blood stain her perfect porcelain skin. He would also lock her up, and eventually she killed herself by refusing to eat anything.

To make things worse, he didn't even care... However, she rose from the grave seeking vengeance and after killing her father; found her husband in bed with a new woman and killed him and then started eating his heart, becoming a vampire. It is believed she still wants revenge on men for the way she was mistreated."

"That's correct; however, it is no legend. The Dearg Due is real and has returned, once again attacking men," Professor Fargo said, impressed with Circe's knowledge.

"So, all myths are real?" Siobhán asked.

"All myths have a basis in reality; however, the truth can be distorted over time. So, how real a myth is, depends on the story in question," Professor Fargo explained.

"So, how are we supposed to stop her?" Brendan asked.

"We put rocks on her grave, so she can't get out," said Patrick joking.

"That's stupid," said Aoife.

"Actually, according to the legend that's how you are supposed to stop her, the problem is that she is supposed to be buried under Strongbow's tree, but no-one has any idea of where that is," Circe said.

"Indeed, we have two choices, we can try and capture the Dearg Due and hope we can reform her. The other option is to destroy her," Professor Fargo said.

"But isn't she a victim, given what happened to her. Is destroying her, really the only opinion," asked Siobhán.

"I think she lost all sympathy when she started killing people and eating their hearts," Dermot said.

"Still…"

"She has to be stopped before more innocent citizens are harmed," Alex said, "Does she have any powers?"

"None have really been mentioned. Though given she eat a heart, suggests she might have super strength," Circe said, trying to remember.

"She probably has all the usual vampire powers," Patrick said, "You know, flight, super strength, maybe some shape-shifting, that sort of stuff."

"Never assume an opponent's powers. That can lead to underestimating them and that could get you or others killed," Professor Fargo warned.

"Are we going to have any actual hero support or are we on our own for this?" Dermot asked as they rest of the class were now realising, they might be doing this without any backup except for the Guardsmen.

"I will be there, and I'll try to gather some more heroes but you are the heroes that have been assigned to stopping the Dearg Due," Professor Fargo said, he knew it wasn't what they wanted to here and he didn't like it either.

Soon a plan was formulated, which wasn't what they wanted to hear. As the Dearg Due was after men, Patrick, Dermot, Brendan, Declan and Professor Fargo would act as bait, while the ladies and Guardsman would keep watch. Then when the Dearg Due appeared, they would have to quickly defeat her. The streets would be clear of all other people to prevent civilians from being put at risk. Also, everyone would not wear their costumes otherwise it would tip her off. Later that night the plan was put into action, everyone was given a communication earpiece so they could all stay in touch…

"I don't like this," Circe said over the communication network.

"None of us do," Aoife said

"At least you and Alex can summon your hero outfits, if necessary, we are sitting ducks," Brendan said.

"At least you can control your powers without yours," Circe said.

"Yeah, so you can protect yourself," Alex said, siding with Circe.

"Concentrate people, we have a vampire to stop," Professor Fargo said.

"Sorry Professor!" They all said.

Professor Fargo knew it was nerves. This was their first mission; they hadn't finishing training and yet were now expected to keep their fellow students safe and stop a centuries old vampire. There was a fear that they could mess up and one of them could end up injured or worse. He even wished he did manage to get some more backup but that didn't happen. Soon there was a sighting.

"Look alive, Brendan, seems you have gotten her attention," Alex said, spotting the Dearg Due heading towards Brendan.

"Moving into position." Everyone else said in unison.

Meanwhile Brendan saw the Dearg Due approach him. She was beautiful, of course if you didn't know what she truly was, you would easily fall for her. He knew the plan, but he didn't want to get bitten. He was ready to blast her with his optic blasts if necessary.

"Excuse me, can you help me?" She said, sounding as innocent and as vulnerable as she could; "My boyfriend just left me and now I have no-one to take me home. Could you please escort me? I'm scared to walk these streets alone."

"That was rather mean of him," Brendan said, trying to stall for time, "How far is it to your place?"

"It isn't too far to walk, if you don't mind?"

"It will be my pleasure," Brendan said, noticing the others arriving and quickly fired an optic blast at the Dearg Due.

"Athrú!" Circe said, transforming into her costume.

"Still wish I had a transformation code," Alex said as her armour emerged around her.

"You don't need one," Circe said as both she and Alex fired blasts at the Dearg Due.

"How dare you!" The Dearg Due screamed, revealing her vampire form.

Circe, Alex and Brendan kept up their attacks to injure and keep her off balance. Then Dermot, grew to increase his strength and punched her straight towards Declan, who quickly grabbed her and rushed her into a dead end. With her cornered the heroes in training were acting more like heroes. Patrick started to shoot electricity at her, to hopefully stun her as Circe, Alex and Brendan arrived along with Siobhán who made it rain to enhance Patrick's electricity. Aoife stood behind the others and used her light to blind the Dearg Due without blinding the others. Professor Fargo arrived along with the Guardsmen; the constant barrage of attacks had weakened the vampire.

"Please, spare me!" she screamed in pain.

"Begging for mercy when you showed none. That's rich," Alex said.

"Please, it's the bloodlust. I can't control it!"

The Dearg Due was desperate, she knew she was trapped. However, she had one trick left; she gathered whatever strength she had left and transformed herself into a mist.

"Where did she go?" Brendan asked the question on everyone's mind.

"Did she teleport?" Siobhán asked.

"Can she do that?" Aoife asked confused.

"She could have turned to mist; some vampires can do that," Patrick said.

"Poor little children, thinking you are heroes but a little trick has confused and scared you. You will pay for daring to strike me, but who?" The Dearg Due thought to herself, still in mist form.

She should just escape while they were confused, but as always, her desire for revenge was stronger. She wanted to make them pay. As a mist, she could move around them all and sense their blood.

"Stay focused, she maybe still around. Alex, Circe, Guardsmen, start scanning the area. Everyone else, keep vigilant" Professor Faro said, also using his own magic to try and detect the Dearg Due.

"A witch, maybe," The Dearg Due thought to herself sensing Siobhán blood, "Maybe the one I was going to attack…"

She approached Brendan, but quickly recalled from him. His blood was tainted, almost inhuman. She quickly moved on and both Alex and Circe and was intrigued by both.

"Blue and Gold blood, both are so tempting," She thought herself, but the power flowing through Circe's veins was too tempting, also she wouldn't have to try and circumnavigate Alex's armour.

She moved around Alex hoping to get closer to Circe when Circe turned and fired an energy blast in Alex's direction. The blast stuck both Alex and the Dearg Due, however due to the nature of Circe's blasts only the Dearg Due was injured.

"What the?" Alex said, shocked that Circe fired at her, and then noticed the Dearg Due lying just beside her.

"I managed to see her near you. Sorry if I scared you," Circe said, apologising.

"It isn't everyday your friend shoots at you," Alex said, getting over the shock.

"True but remember my blasts couldn't hurt you since you weren't a threat and you are a friend."

"I know, still you saved my life. I don't know how to repay you."

"You don't have to."

"But I must."

"Alex, it's okay. Besides, is she dead?"

The Dearg Due lay on the ground, her strength gone. The heroes gathered around her. She begged for her life once more. Professor Fargo looked at the vampire as she begged and did what they all agreed to do. With a gesture of his staff, she was frozen in place allowing the Guardsmen to arrest her.

"Everyone is allowed the right to a fair trial," he said as they had all agreed.

While originally, some had believed that destroying the vampire was the only way, a hero should save lives, not destroy them, even monsters. Maybe she could be rehabilitated, time would tell but at least she had been stopped. As the Guardsmen took her to a containment facility, Professor Fargo addressed his students.

"Thank you all for your amazing work. You acted like full-fledged heroes, despite the strange circumstances. You should all be proud of what you achieved. I'll deal with the paperwork. You all head home and get some rest and because of your efforts, there will be no classes tomorrow."

"Thank you, Professor Fargo." They all said, delighted to have helped and for the whole adventure to be over.

As the students began to head home. Alex took Circe aside.

"You saved my life," Alex said

"Alex, I said it is okay. You don't have to repay me or anything. We are training to be heroes, saving lives is what we do, or will be doing," Circe said modestly, "Now that the Dearg Due has been stopped, we should head home. What are you going to do? I doubt there are any trains this late."

"I booked into a hotel. Still, I will find a way of repaying you."

"It's okay. You don't need to feel indebted to me."

Alex knew she wasn't going to be able to change Circe's mind; so, she decided to drop the subject for now. As it was late, the Guardsmen offered all the heroes in training a lift home or to their hotel. Circe arrived home and was quickly greeted by her dad.

"Are you okay?" he asked.

"I'm fine dad. Wait have you been up waiting?" Circe said a bit surprised.

"Well, I wouldn't be a good parent, if I wasn't up worrying about my daughter."

"Dad!" she said, hugging him.

"I know, I shouldn't, but it doesn't matter if you have powers or not, 17 or 700, I will always be concerned for your safety. So, how did it go?"

Despite the late hour, Circe told her dad about what happened. Meanwhile, Alex was doing likewise with her father over the phone in her hotel room.

"We have a problem," Alex said

"You said there wouldn't be any problems." Her father said sternly.

"The identity is fine, but during tonight's mission Circe saved my life."

"She's the demi-goddess you mention quite a bit."

"I am not sure she is a demi-goddess, but yeah she is the one"

"You know what that means, my daughter."

"I know, but the problem is she would not accept that I owe her anything."

"So, you are indebted to her, but she does not know how serious that is."

"That is a tricky one," Her mother entered the conversation.

"Indeed Mother, I cannot force her to accept and I cannot really do anything without exposing myself."

"Let your father and I think about it. You enjoy your day off." Her mother said.

"Don't you want me back in Kingdom City?"

"It is fine. You helped save lives and deserve a break. We will see you tomorrow evening." Her father said.

"Very well. Good Night Father, Good Night Mother," she said as she ended the call, being a hero with a secret wasn't easy.

The next day Circe was in her room trying to figure out what to do with her day off. Most of her friends were on various holidays or working. She was trying to figure out what to do when her dad entered.

"Everything okay?"

"Yeah Dad. Just trying to think what to do," she said, usually the two would plan if they both wanted to do something.

"Well, since you have the day off, you can see that movie you wanted to see," he said.

"You're right. I thought I wouldn't be able to see it since I had classes but since I don't, I can see it," Circe said excited. "Do you want to come?"

"Nah, I have some things to do around the school, besides, it isn't my kind of movie."

"You never were one for the historical movies."

"True."

"Still, it would be strange to go on my own."

"Isn't Alex still in town, why don't you ask her?"

Circe quickly rang Alex.

"Which movie is it?" Alex asked.

"It's a classic movie about the sinking of a ship."

"Is that the one with the love story?"

"No, it's the original version, black and white and everything."

"Don't think I've seen that one. Sounds like fun."

"Great I'll meet you at your hotel and then we can head to the theatre."

"Ohh, is this a date?" Alex said half-jokingly.

"Maybe we should see how this goes first," Circe said, also half-jokingly.

After getting ready, Circe walked into the city to meet Alex. She really hoped Alex wouldn't mention the whole saving her life and therefore being indebted thing. She soon arrived at the hotel and it wasn't too long before Alex appeared.

"Wow, you look amazing" Alex said, complimenting Circe.

"Thanks, you look great yourself."

"Why thank you. Since you know where we are going you better lead the way."

The two ladies headed through an archway and towards a large building.

"This isn't Sunsport's cinema, is it?" Alex asked.

"Actually, we have two, this is an arts centre which does show classic movies from time to time. They also have exhibitions and plays," Circe explained.

The two entered the building and got their tickets, while waiting for the doors to open, they decided to check out the art exhibitions in the centre. After admiring the artworks, the two headed in to see the classic movie. It was a treat for both of them; for Circe seeing one of her favourite films on the big screen was amazing; for Alex watch it for the first time and being able to share it with her friend. After the movie, the two spent the day together until it was time for Alex to head home.

"That's it, you have to come to Kingdom City so I can show you around," Alex said.

"I would love that. We should definitely arrange something," Circe said, already liking the idea.

"Fantastic, well see you next week," Alex said as she headed to catch her train.

As Alex boarded her train, she called her parents.

"Hello Father, hello Mother."

"How was your day?" her father asked.

Alex excitedly told her parents about the time she spent with Circe and that she hoped to show Circe around Kingdom City.

"It might be tricky, but it is something we can discuss, still we have that other matter with your friend to deal with," her father said.

"So, you have an idea."

"We do, but you may not like it," her mother said, "we will brief you when you return."

Alex was concerned about what her parents had planned, but she hoped it would help her predicament.

Soon a new day approached and the heroes in training where told not to go to the school but instead to the theatre that Circe and Alex had gone to. The heroes in training were confused for the second time in recent days and they didn't like it, especially as they were also told to wear their costumes. They all gathered however they noticed Alex was missing.

"Hey, where's Alex?" Siobhán said, quickly noticing.

"Her mum's sick, so she's looking after her," Circe explained having gotten a text from Alex earlier.

"I hope she gets better," said Siobhán.

"So do I," said Circe.

"Ah, you are all here, barring Ms Clúdach, but she did inform me she would be absent today. Still, it would have been preferable to have you all," said Professor Fargo as he greeted the heroes in training. "I have to apologise for this change in both location and schedule but it was a request I couldn't refuse."

Professor Fargo led them inside. The place seemed largely deserted. There was some voices but nothing else. The group was led to the theatre area and asked to stand on the stage and then Professor Fargo left. The heroes in training were getting more confused by the minute. Soon Professor Fargo returned, but with a very special guest. To their surprise, he was accompanied by Princess Edelgard. The Princess was wearing a simple white dress with short sleeves with a blue coat and belt. Her jewellery was just as simple, with a broach and some bracelets. While her outfit was simple, her aura and presence was undeniable royal.

"So, these are the young heroes that stopped the Dearg Due?" She asked Professor Fargo.

"Yes, your Highness, we have Brendan Ross, Dermot McGrath, Siobhán Regan, Declan Walsh, Aoife McCarthy, Patrick Deasy and Circe Goodwin," Professor Fargo said, introducing each of the heroes in training to the princess.

"I was informed there are eight heroes in training." The princess asked.

"Sadly, Alex Clúdach's mother is ill and so she's looking after her," Professor Fargo explained.

"A shame, I will have to thank her later, if you would be so kind as to tell me her address," The Princess said.

They couldn't believe it, as she shook each of their hands and briefly talked to them. As she shook Circe's hand, Circe could help but feel there was something familiar about her. Then her precognitive powers activated and warned her.

"BOMB!" She shouted.

Everyone was startled as Circe grabbed the Princess and tried to shield her with her body as a bomb went off somewhere near the theatre. The explosion rocked the theatre causing a stage light to fall heading directly above Circe and the Princess. Professor Fargo tried to reach the two ladies, however Circe quickly noticed it and reacted by firing a blast at it causing it to vaporise.

"Are you two, okay?" Professor Fargo asked.

"I'm fine," Circe said, getting to her feet, "Are you okay Your Highness?"

The Princess was still curled in a ball.

"WhydidithavetobeabombIhateexplosionstheyknewthato fcoursetheyknewthat" The Princess said, rambling and scared with tears in her eye.

"Your Highness, the threat is over," Professor Fargo said, receiving some news from the earpiece he was wearing.

Princess Edelgard looked up at Professor Fargo and Circe and looked as they both nodded. Circe helped her to her feet, and she wiped away the tears from her eye, which confused Circe as why she wasn't wiping both eyes. After a minute, the Princess regarded her composure.

"I am fine now. Ms Goodwin, you saved my life, I am in your debt."

"It was nothing. You don't have to feel indebted to me, I was just doing what anyone else would have done," Circe said, she had heard the same thing from Alex, royalty or not she didn't want anyone to be indebted.

"Such modesty, "The Princess said with a smile, "However, saving my life means I owe you an Honour Debt. It is my royal obligation to repay you and is something that I cannot ignore. Whether you like it or not, you have a royal in your debt."

Her demeanour was serious yet grateful. It was also like she was glad to be indebted to her. There was more to the Princess than met the eye, but Circe wasn't going to pry.

"Now Professor about that bomb…"

"The Guardsmen are already dealing with it. I have also been informed that there was no casualties or fatalities," Professor Fargo reported.

"I would appear to have been the target, but this was arranged quite quickly and secretly. Hopefully, there isn't a security breach either at the castle or your school. However, if I was the target, the bomb should have been better placed. Still, I hope to get answers soon enough," The Princess said, trying to make sense of the attack.

"Maybe we should get you to somewhere safer, just in case there is another attack," Circe suggested.

"A wise suggestion, also I would be honoured Ms Goodwin if you and your family come to the Castle as my personal guests this weekend. My parents would be very interested to meet the lady who saved my life," The Princess said as Professor Fargo decided to take her to safety.

"I would suggest you all head home, just in case," Professor Fargo said to all the heroes in training.

"A royal invite! That's amazing Circe!" Aoife said before they departed.

"You are going to have to tell us all about it," Siobhán said.

"How did you know about the bomb" Brendan asked.

"According to Professor Fargo, I have limited precognitive abilities. I could see an image of the explosion, but it doesn't happen all the time."

"If you get the Lotto numbers let us know," Dermot said half-jokingly.

"So far, it only seems to be for threats, but you never know."

As the group disbanded Circe headed home, she did find it strange that despite the bomb blast there wasn't any real commotion. Was there a bomb? They heard and felt the explosion but there doesn't seem to be anything strange. Maybe the Guardsmen quickly cleared the area? She arrived home, her dad was out getting some groceries. She had already rung him to check that he was okay. In her room she decided to see how Alex was.

"You met the Princess? Oh, I am so jealous!" Alex said over the phone.

"I'm sorry you missed her. How is your mum?"

"She better, a bit of food poisoning, so hopefully I'll be back tomorrow. Still how was the Princess? Was she really sexy?"

"She is really attractive. I have to say you look a bit like her."

"So, you think I'm really attractive. Circe, a lot of teenagers up here resemble the Princess. She's extremely popular so everyone tries to copy her style. When you come to Kingdom City, you will be seeing a lot of ladies with hair covering an eye."

"Speaking of going to Kingdom City, I'll be up this weekend. You see I saved the Princess's life and now she indebted to me, even though I don't want her to.

"That's two people's lives you have saved. Maybe your hero name could be Lifesaver. You still haven't said how I can repay you."

"Alex, you don't have to be indebted to me, you can't invoke an Honour Debt like the Princess did."

"So, she's legally bound to repay you. I should have thought of that."

"Thankfully, you didn't"

"What does your dad think?"

"I haven't told him everything yet. I only briefly rang him to check to see if he was okay following the bomb attack."

"I just heard about that on the news. Thankfully, no-one was hurt."

"Yeah, hopefully they will catch the people responsible."

"I'm sure they will. I have to go; my mum is calling me."

"Okay, I'll hopefully see you tomorrow."

Circe hung up and decided to do some drawing to pass the time. Soon her dad returned with the groceries. She helped him put them away, while explaining everything that happened.

"Are you sure you are okay?" Her dad said, concerned that his daughter was near an explosion and almost had a light fall on her.

"Dad, I'm fine, not even a scratch." Circe quickly showed to alleviate her dad's concerns.

"I am so proud of you," he said, hugging her.

"Thanks dad. I'm still not keen on someone thinking that they have to owe me anything."

"With a Princess in our corner, we would be set for life," her father said jokingly.

"Dad!"

"I was only kidding. Still, something like an Honour Debt isn't something to squander either."

"I know."

"Still, we better start figuring out what we are supposed to do about this royal invite. Hopefully, we will get more details."

"Maybe there is some details online."

"Wouldn't hurt checking."

Circe headed to one of the school's computer labs to use the internet. The school wouldn't allow Wi-Fi as they feared all the students would be all the time on their phones instead of learning. Even she and her dad had pushed for the school to update the school's internet policy but they were stuck in their ways. As she began her search, she noticed an email. It was from Kingdom Castle itself. She was confused on how they got her email, maybe Professor Fargo gave it to the Princess after they left, but even if it was a request from a royal, he should have at least asked. Still the email contained all the details they were looking for. Everything from times, dress sense, what they could and couldn't do, it was very well detailed and easy to understand. She printed out all the details, making a note of her usage and headed back to her dad.

"Well, this is very comprehensive, though I would like to know how they got your email," her dad said, looking at the details.

"It is a bit concerning" Circe said, "Still they probably just asked someone like Professor Fargo."

Soon the date with royalty arrived. As they headed towards the Castle, Circe saw Alex was right about the amount of people imitating the Princess's hairstyle.

"I knew she was popular and a style icon but this is insane," David said.

"I thought Alex was joking but look at them all," Circe said in amazement.

"Don't start getting any ideas."

"You don't think, I would look lovely with my hair styled over my eye?"

"You are lovely the way you are."

"Thanks Dad. Let's see we are supposed to turn left here," Circe said with a smile before focusing on the directions they had been given.

The direction took them to a small side gate to the castle away from the main entrance. However, there was a Royal Guardsman there.

"Can I help you?" He asked in a serious but polite manner.

"I'm David Goodwin and this is my daughter Circe, we have a Royal Invite for dinner," David said, slightly worried but showed the Royal Guardsmen the email.

The Royal Guardsman checked a device on his wristband against the email..

"You are cleared, follow the road up and park on the right," he said as the gate opened.

The small road led through part of the Castle grounds. The grounds were massive, it was hard to believe something like this was in a city. Soon they parked the car and were greeted by two Royal Guardsmen.

"I hope we look alright," Circe said.

She was wearing the dress she had gotten for her birthday, with matching shoes. Her dad was wearing his best suit. Both felt, no matter how they looked they were underdressed.

"You look stunning," her dad said, reassuring her.

"Thanks Dad."

The two were brought through the main doors of the Castle. The two looked in amazement, despite working and living in a former castle, Kingdom Castle looked made St.

Declan's Castle look like their actual apartment. They were soon greeted by Princess Edelgard, she was wearing a blue top, a blue skirt, a white sleeveless undershirt, a white dress and a pair of white gloves all with gold trim and gold belt, with various pieces of jewellery and topped with her tiara. Both Goodwins bowed in front of the Princess.

"Circe, I am so glad you accepted my invitation," Princess Edelgard said with delight, "and this I assume is your father."

"You assume correctly, your Highness. I am David Goodwin. It is an honour to be invited," David said politely.

"The honour is mine, Mr Goodwin, now we must head to the dining hall. My father likes things to be on time, even dinner. So please, follow me."

The Princess guided the Goodwins through the Castle. It was a good thing they had a guide as it seemed it would be easy to get lost.

"I must say Circe, I love your dress," The Princess said with a huge smile.

"Why thank you, your Highness, but it is nothing compared to yours."

"Nonsense, you look amazing and here we are," The Princess said as she opened the doors to a large room.

Inside was a very large dining hall where King Brian and Queen Sarah were already waiting. Both approached the Goodwins who bowed before them.

"Father, Mother, may I present Circe Goodwin and her father David," Princess Edelgard said to her parents.

"Welcome to our humble home," said Queen Sarah, "Now please sit and we can begin the meal."

The five sat down. King Brian was at the head of the table, with Queen Sarah and Princess Edelgard sitting on either side,

Circe sat next to the Princess while David sat next to the Queen. Both Goodwins were nervous about sitting next to royalty, but the royal family did their best to ease their nerves, Princess Edelgard seemed to like the idea of Circe sitting next to her.

"Thank you so much for saving Edelgard's life. She means the world to us and we would be lost if anything were to happen to her," King Brian said, full of gratitude.

"It was nothing, Your Majesty. I just did what I was trained to do," Circe said politely.

"You were right, she is very modest," Queen Sarah said to Princess Edelgard.

Getting all this praise caused Circe to blush.

"So, David how long have you been a single parent? If you don't mind me asking," King Brian said.

"Since she was a baby. I took her in and I never once looked back," David said proudly.

"Took her in?" Queen Sarah interest was piqued by the statement.

"Circe is my adopted daughter," David said, explaining.

"I see. To take on that much responsibility on your own, shows where your daughter's character come from," Queen Sarah said, impressed.

"Thank you Your Majesty."

"Circe's power was amazing. Somehow she knew there was an attack going to happen and managed to protect me. Then a stage light threatened to fall on us and she vaporised it," Princess Edelgard said, recalling the events.

"Of course, they would be amazing as they were Divine. Gods don't give standard powers," King Brian stated.

This caused confused looks from both Goodwins and a death glare from the Princess.

"Excuse me, Your Majesty, but how do you know my powers are Divine?" Circe asked.

"It was a guess," King Brian said with certainty though he acted nervous.

"Really Father? You seemed so certain," Princess Edelgard said, clearly angry or annoyed.

"Of course, it was a guess. The way you described it made it sound like you were rescued by a Guardian Angel."

"If you say so, Father."

The last thing this dinner needed was a Royal family argument in front of their guests. Neither Goodwin wanted to press the topic further in case the anger the Royal family, so, they continued eating and chatting.

"So, Circe, what powers do you have? Edelgard has described them as best as she could, but it would be nice to hear from the source," Queen Sarah asked.

"Well, I can fire energy blasts from my hands which seem to only affect things that threated me or anyone I'm trying to protect.. I can see invisible objects and I have limited precognitive abilities which I have little control over. Also, I can make my hero costume magically appear and disappear at will," Circe said, trying her best to explain her powers.

"You should see her costume Mother; it is really pretty," Princess Edelgard said.

"Maybe after dinner," Queen Sarah said.

The dinner continued without any more strange statements. Afterwards Circe showed the Royal Family her costume. Then Princess Edelgard decided to take Circe on a tour of the castle.

"I hope you enjoy history, otherwise this is going to be a very bad tour," Princess Edelgard said with some nerves.

"I love history it is my favourite subject," Circe said, excited at possibly seeing some rare artefacts.

"I had a feeling you would say that, so let's begin."

"Lead the way Your Highness."

Princess Edelgard stopped and made a deep sigh.

"Is everything okay?" Circe asked concerned.

"It is always Your Highness," Princess Edelgard said, upset under her breath.

"I'm sorry?" Circe's concern now changed to confusion.

Had she upset the Princess somehow? She followed the protocol laid out in the invite.

"Circe, could you please call me by my name not any of my titles from now on?"

"I can't do that! That would be improper!" Circe said, shocked. She had no right to refer to the Princess by her name.

"It is okay; I am giving you permission. The only people that ever call me by my name are my family, everyone else uses a title and I hate it. It makes me sound less of a person. So, as your princess I want you to always call me by my name," The Princess said with compassion and even handing her a special letter stating it.

"Very well.... Edelgard," Circe said nervously and looking at the Royal letter.

"My name is not that hard to pronounce. Now on with this tour," Edelgard said almost like a different person, like a weight had been lifted. Her attitude seemed familiar...

Edelgard took Circe into a large room full of tapestries. Circe looked in amazement at all of them. She had seen them in photos and on TV but never in the flesh.

"This tapestries in this hall tell the history of Hibernia. We start with this one, this sees the three Goddesses Banba, Ériu and Fódla meeting the bard Amergin. Each Goddess wanted the island to be named after her and they asked Amergin to decide. He asked them to each predict the future and the most accurate who have the land named after them."

"It was Ériu, as the Gaelic for Hibernia is Eire. By the way which is which?" Circe said, remembering her books on mythology.

"You are correct that Ériu won. That one is Banba, Ériu is that one and Fódla is the farthest one."

"She has purple eyes," Circe said, looking at the tapestry.

"Who?" Edelgard said, wondering what Circe was talking about.

"Ériu, it could be artistic license but if that's the case why?"

"I never noticed that. It seems strange for someone to be giving purple eyes on a tapestry, but these tapestries are known to have deliberate faults. Still let us move on"

The two continued through the tapestries when one of them caught Circe's eye. Edelgard quickly noticed Circe's interest.

"This one shows the Fomorian King Balor's defeat at the hands of his own grandson Lug. It is said after the battle, Balor's body was cut into pieces by his own sword and scattered across the land."

"Was that the sword that was stolen from the museum? It was called the Blade of Balor?" Circe said, remembering the theft.

"I'm not sure if it is the same sword, it could be. My Father would probably know," Edelgard said, thinking about it.

The tour continued with both ladies enjoying every moment. Eventually they returned to their parents. Soon the Goodwins had to leave. As they headed home, David noticed Circe was deep in thought.

"Everything okay?" he asked.

"Yeah I was just thinking of something I saw on the tour."

"Oh, what's that?"

"Well, Edelgard," Circe said, starting to explain.

"Circe, you can't call the Princess by her name!" David said, shocked.

"Actually, she wanted me to. She even gave me a Royal letter saying so."

"Okay, so what about the tour?"

"She was showing me, this room full of tapestries depicting Hibernia's history and one of them showed how Hibernia got its original name."

"Ah with the three sisters, I remember reading you that story and many others, when you were little."

"Yeah, they were great. Anyway, the tapestry depicted Ériu with purple eyes. Edelgard said that the artists were known to deliberately add in mistakes but why the eye colour?"

"I'm guessing there is more to this than just artist licence."

"Yeah, you remember why Ériu won?"

"She made the most accurate prediction..." David said before realising what Circe was saying.

"A goddess with precognition and purple eyes, sounds familiar?"

"I admit it does remind me of when you are in your costume, but do you really think that she could be responsible for your powers?"

"I don't know, but it is the first time we might have gotten even a clue to why I have these powers."

"It might tell us where or who you got them from but we are no closer to actually knowing why they were given to you. I doubt you are going to be asked to make a prediction in order to get a country named after you."

"Probably not. It's annoying just when I might have an answer it just leads to more questions," Circe said a bit frustrated.

"Hey, Hey. We have something at least; it is speculation but it is something we could look into. Besides, we shouldn't let this ruin what was a very special day."

"You're right, Dad!"

As the two continued on their journey home, it was just another road on the journey of Circe's life.

Chapter 5
I'm Off to Betray You, Goodbye

The sun was shining over Sunsport and Circe was outside the front of St. Declan's. In front of her were some makeshift targets with a deep breathe, she attempted to fire at them. With all her training a few weak powered blasts came from her fingers, doing little damage to the targets.

"I'm pretty sure your blasts are more powerful than that," David said, watching his daughter.

"They are, when I transform."

"So, transform and blast them."

"That's easy. I'm trying to use my powers when I'm not transformed. So far, it is a lot harder."

"Well, you have improved, remember when it just flopped out of your hand?"

"Which you recorded, so we'll never forget."

"It is still hard to believe how much things have changed since then."

He was right, things had changed. She had gone from a simple schoolgirl who lived with her dad, to being a hero in training and recently a friend of the Princess of Hibernia. Despite all the changes she was still no closer to learning how or why she had gotten her powers.

"I'm going to practice some more," she said as she charged up for another blast.

"Okay, just don't overdo it."

As her dad was about to head inside, Circe made a weird noise and collapsed.

"Circe? CIRCE!" He rushed over to his daughter as he did, Circe began to open her eyes.

"What happened?" She asked a bit groggy.

"I was about to ask you. Are you okay?"

"I'm okay, I had another vision, I think."

"The last time didn't knock you out."

"I was sleeping the last time. Still, this was just as frightening. There were like an army of these weird creatures. They had one eye, one arm and one leg and they were attacking everywhere. A whole group of them swarmed around me and then there was like a flash and that was it," she said, clearly shaken.

"Let's go inside and try to relax."

Inside, David gave her daughter some hot chocolate, which helped calm her down.

"I could really do without these visions," she said.

"Well, we haven't been attacked by a Cyclops yet."

"That's what's worries me. I had that nightmare/vision of Balor and nothing. I have no clue how far into the future I'm seeing. Still maybe I should try and find out what those creatures were."

"Are you sure, you are okay?"

"I'm just going to look at some books."

"Still take it easy."

In her room Circe was trying to figure out where to start with her vision. The creatures she saw didn't look or sound familiar. As she looked at her books, she heard a familiar disembodied voice.

"Start with your last vision, but please be careful, not everyone is what they seem."

"Okay, who are you?" Circe said but she got no answer.

"Circe, is everything okay?" Her father said, concerned.

"I heard that voice again, it seemed to be trying to warn me, that not everyone is what they seem."

"That's vague and ominous like your visions."

"Yeah, still it said I should start with my last vision."

"Are you sure we should be trusting the ghost?"

"So far it hasn't done anything to harm us."

Circe looked at her book of Irish myths and legends and next to the story of Balor was a picture of a Fomorian which resembled what she had seen in her vision. Things were getting scary, two visions about Balor and around the time her powers emerged there was a theft of a weapon with his name. Could they be linked? Something was telling her they must be. Ancient gods, powers, ghosts, none of it made sense, why was this happening to her?

"Everything okay?"

"Yeah dad, just trying to figure out what these visions mean. I think they are linked to that theft at the New Helvetica Museum."

"It seems that way, but it doesn't explain what it has to do with you."

"I wish I knew."

That night Circe was finding it hard to sleep. Her mind was full of questions and no answers. However, when she did finally fall asleep, it wasn't peaceful. Another vision entered her mind. She couldn't move, there was someone with a strange blade, she couldn't move or even make a sound, the blade pierced her and she woke up screaming.

"Circe, what's wrong?" her dad rushed in after hearing her scream.

"I think I had another vision. I think I just saw my death," she said with tears in her eyes.

She explained what she had seen, how she felt helpless. Her dad comforted her.

"Shh, it's okay. No-one is going to stab you. As we talked about earlier, it could never happen."

He spent a good part of the night comforting her. Circe was almost terrified of going back to sleep in case she got another vision. When she finally did fall asleep, he stayed by her side just in case. The next day meant another week of training and Circe did her best to shake off the horrible visions she had gotten the day before. Seeing Alex really helped. Alex wanted to hear all about Circe meeting the Princess.

"She must really like you if she allowed you not to called her by a title," Alex said.

"I was surprised but I can't really ignore a request from the Princess."

"No, you cannot," Alex said with a smile, "By the way are you okay? You look exhausted."

Circe filled her in on the two visions she had.

"Yikes, I'm glad I don't have that power."

"I wish I didn't have it either."

"Come on or we are going to be late. Hopefully, this class won't be too stressful."

"It's Power Theory, so it shouldn't be too bad."

After class, Circe went to Professor Fargo's office. She entered to see once again Professor Fargo and Hex Queen talking about the theft at the New Helvetica Museum. It seemed that the culprit did a really good job of covering their tracks. As the two welcomed her in Circe noticed the picture of the Blade of Balor.

"That's it!"

"What's it? You're not making any sense," Hex Queen said.

Circe filled both teachers on her visions.

"A vison about an attack by Fomorians and being attacked by the Blade that he owned and was used to kill him," Professor Fargo said, thinking out loud.

"It wasn't just being attacked; I could feel the blade piercing my..." Circe was about to break down just remembering the vision by being stabbed in the heart when both teachers comforted her.

"It's okay Circe, these visions can be horrifying but they might have given us a clue to the thief's intention and why you have your powers," Professor Fargo said.

"I don't understand."

"I believe the thief is going to try and resurrect Balor."

"Wait, Fargo are you sure?" Hex Queen said, shocked that Professor Fargo would suggest that.

"Sadly, it makes sense, Vivian. The Blade of Balor is a weapon used in Necromancy. With Circe's visions of a Fomorian attack, I believe it is safe to say that the Fomorians are back and trying to revive their king"

"But why now? The Blade of Balor has been at the museum for years," Hex Queen asked.

"Because she had her awakening, you suspected that Circe's powers activated due to what was going to happen. As it seems you may be right, she might be connected to the Fomorian's plans."

"But in what way? I didn't ask for these powers," Circe said, she wasn't liking Professor Fargo's train of thought.

"That we don't know. The Blade of Balor is cleared designed as a necromantic artefact. However, without any details on the actual ritual, it is hard to say how you are truly connected. There are too many unknowns."

"Maybe there is something we can do," Hex Queen said, thinking of something.

"What?" Circe was now curious.

"A mystical blood test," Hex Queen stated.

"A blood test?"

"A mystical blood test, Ms Goodwin. We would take a small sample of your blood and try to determine what properties it has. It could give us a better idea on your powers and how they might be used in a ritual," Hex Queen explained.

"Of course, the decision is yours."

"If it gets me some answers, I'll do it."

The two teachers took Circe to Hex Queen's office. She got a small box from her desk which contained a small medical case. She pricked Circe's finger causing a small drop of blood to fall on a small plate. After cleaning the small wound, Hex Queen placed the plate on the floor and began to gesture her arms to perform a magic spell. However, what was supposed to be a simple spell, she seemed to be struggling.

"What's wrong?" Professor Fargo asked concerned.

"I'm not sure, there seems to be something preventing me from reading her blood," Hex Queen said, confused as it was like something was trying to stop her from completing her spell.

Suddenly there was a flash of fuchsia energy from the blood which sent Hex Queen into the wall.

"Vivian!" Professor Fargo rushed over with Circe doing likewise.

"I'm okay," Hex Queen said as Professor Fargo helped her up.

Circe looked horrified and upset that her powers had sent another teacher flying.

"It's not your fault," Hex Queen said, noticing Circe's expression. "You didn't mystically protect your blood.

"But"

"No buts, clearly this was done to prevent anyone trying to learn anything about your blood. I suspect to protect you. However, this hasn't been a failure, this reaction means that you blood is very special and along with your visions suggest that you are important to the Fomorians' plot," Hex Queen said.

"Unfortunately, this also means you are in great danger," Professor Fargo said.

"What?"

"Given your visions and what we now know, I sadly believe that the Fomorians will try and sacrifice you as part of a ritual to revive Balor," Professor Fargo said in a very serious tone.

"Sadly, I have to agree. What about her father? Could he be targeted?" Hex Queen asked.

"I doubt it. When we tried the Omen Orb it didn't react to him at all."

"The Omen Orb can be manipulated."

"If he was a very powerful being but Circe's father isn't her father."

"You mean?"

"I'm adopted," Circe said, explaining to Hex Queen. "According to my dad, I was abandoned on the doorstep of St. Declan's Castle. Though, there was a note left with me and a book."

"I know it is personal, but what was the note and the book?" Professor Fargo asked. Asking Circe about her adoption was something he would normally try to avoid, as it was a personal and sensitive subject but since she brought it up, she was felt it could be important.

"The book was Osborn's book of Greek Myths and the note said 'Choose a name from this book and keep her safe'," Circe said.

"Well, that explains your Greek name, but the note also suggests that whoever left you there, was trying to protect you from something, maybe even this threat," Professor Fargo said.

"Not sure why they would want you to be named after someone in Greek Mythology?" Hex Queen said, confused.

"I think my name is the least of my problems," Circe said.

"True and it is a lovely name."

"Focus ladies. Due to Circe's visions, we have learned that the Fomorians are planning a return and are planning to revive their king, Balor. Circe seems to be critical to the resurrection ritual."

"Sadly, we don't know when this will happen," Hex Queen said, slightly annoyed.

"So, what do we do?" Circe asked.

"We will try to get more information; you try to focus on your training and living your life. If you have any visions let us know, no matter when they happen. Just try not to let this get you down," Professor Fargo said.

Circe left the office and started to head home. It was a trip she had taken numerous times but with all the talk of monsters and sacrifices, she all of a sudden didn't feel safe. She called her dad and asked him to pick her up.

"Sorry for making you pick me up," she said as she got into the car.

"Nonsense, if my daughter doesn't feel safe then she doesn't feel safe. So, what did Professor Fargo say."

Circe filled her dad in what happened.

"So, you sent another teacher into a wall."

"I didn't mean to and I didn't do it my blood somehow did," Circe said, trying to defend herself.

"I'm only joking."

"Well, it wasn't funny. Dad, I... I'm scared. I'm scared some mythological creatures are going to kill me," Circe said as she began to get upset.

"Damn these visions. Circe, you aren't going to die. You know I'll do anything in my power to protect you."

"I know Dad, it's just hard to shake this off."

Circe spend the rest of the day with her dad, doing her best not to think of her Visions. That night didn't help as she had the same visions. Except they were more vivid. She woke up screaming to see her dad already there.

"How long have you been there..." She said, trying to catch her breath.

"Well, I couldn't sleep either."

"I can't turn them off," Circe said as she started to cry.

"Shhh, it's okay. We'll work through this, as well have with all of your powers," he said, doing everything he could think of to comfort her.

"My other powers don't show me my death."

Following another restless night, it was another day of Power Training. However, the students were in for a surprise. First, they were told to wear their hero costumes and when they arrived in their costumes, they were greeted by not only the teachers but also a large number of small robots.

"Today's training will be a bit different. Today you will be learning how to deal with a large group of villains. You will have to use teamwork to defeat them," Professor Fargo said as he addressed the young heroes in training.

Circe suspected that this training was influenced by her visions. Still, it would also be a test to see if her powers could work on robots. The robots began to charge at the heroes in training. Circe fired off a blast and it destroyed one of them. The others using what they had learned also managed to destroy some of the robots.

"This is easy, "said Patrick delighted to be able to cut loose.

"Hey Circe, I though your powers didn't work on metal?" Brendan asked.

"Do you think I'm complaining," Circe said as she blasted another robot.

"Only if it is pure Iron. Which these robots aren't made of" Professor Fargo explained, "and don't get cocky, you haven't beaten these robots yet."

Just when they had thought they defeated the last robot, the robots rebuilt themselves.

"Wait, what's going on?" Aoife asked.

"They are rebuilding themselves. How are we supposed to beat them?" Siobhán said.

"Stay calm, they have to have a weakness," Alex said with an air of leadership around her. "One of you destroy a robot and I'll scan the parts to see if I can find anything unusual. The rest of you defend me until I'm finished."

Circe quickly destroyed a robot and Alex began her scan. Everyone then prevented any of the robots from attacking her. Soon Alex's scan got her the information she wanted.

"I got something. There is a small silver ball, which contains the regenerative program. We have to destroy that in each robot otherwise they regenerate."

With this new information, the heroes in training started to defeat the robot army. Eventually all the robots were destroyed and were not rebuilding themselves.

"Well done. You have managed to defeat the robot army and in a reasonable time. Since we still have some time left, we will go back to regular training."

As the young heroes in training and their teachers got into their usual training groups, it gave Circe a chance to talk with Professor Fargo.

"The visions seem to be getting worse Professor. I can't turn them off and they are getting more vivid."

"Any more details?"

"Nothing massive, I can start to see whoever is using the Blade of Balor but it's all blurry. I just want them to stop."

"Sadly, dealing with precognition isn't one of my strong points. In fact, we have very few heroes with precognition. Hex Queen might be able to do something to help you sleep, so come by my office later."

After class, Hex Queen managed to give Circe a potion to help her sleep. That night she took a small dose as directed and hoped for a good night sleep. It didn't come. The visions were getting worse. Seeing his daughter being tormented was horrifying for David. He hated feeling powerless to help her. He decided to call Professor Fargo for help. Though it was late at night Professor Fargo and Hex Queen arrived.

"I'm so sorry for calling you this late," David said as he answered the door and invited both teachers in.

The two teachers entered the Circe's room where she was still be tormented by her visions. Hex Queen noticed the small bottle of the sleep potion. Circe had taken the right amount and yet it didn't work. There was more to Circe that met the eye which meant that all of her mystical knowledge might not be good enough.

"Have you tried waking her?" Professor Fargo asked.

"Yes, but I can't wake her."

"I'll try a waking spell. Though if my sleeping potion didn't work, I'm not sure that this will be much good," Hex Queen said, concerned.

She began to gesture her arms to perform the spell when she sensed a presence.

"What's wrong?" David asked concerned.

"Did anyone else sense or feel that?" Hex Queen asked.

"No." Both David and Professor Fargo replied.

"Vivian, what did you sense?" Professor Fargo asked.

"I'm not sure but there seems to be a female presence around."

"Circe has mentioned hearing a female voice which seems to guide her, but we don't know who or what it is. I don't think it's a ghost."

"Well, it's not a ghost. I can tell you that," Professor Fargo said.

"Should we try waking her?" David asked concerned.

"I have a feeling that the presence I felt won't let us," Hex Queen said.

Suddenly Circe woke up shaken from her visions and surprised to see two of her teachers in her room.

"What's going on?" She asked confused and a bit embarrassed.

"You were clearly tormented by more visions, so I called them to try and help you," her father explained.

"I'm sorry my potion didn't help you sleep."

"It's okay Hex Queen, you tried and I'm thankful."

"It looked like the visions were getting worse. I tried to wake you but I couldn't," her dad said, concerned.

"I know I could hear you, but the voice said, 'I'm sorry but you have to know this'."

"What did you see?" Professor Fargo asked.

"It was the same visions, but the army of Fomorians was bigger than before and the person who was stabbing me kept changing into one of my classmates," Circe said, clearly shaken.

"Just try to get some rest. The sleeping potion should still be in your system so hopefully you should be able to get some rest," Hex Queen said.

"If you don't mind, we would like to stay here a bit longer just in case," Professor Fargo said.

David led the two teachers into the living room to try and let Circe get some sleep. He gave them a cup of tea and they all talked about Circe's visions.

"Are these visions ever going to stop? I fear she's going to go insane with them."

"Unfortunately, they will only stop when whatever they are trying to show her passes. Even then, she could get new visions with regards another future event," Professor Fargo said.

"So, it could happen all over again."

"Sadly, it's a possibility," Professor Fargo said.

"Let's deal with these visions first. What is worrying are the changes to both visions. The first one showing the army growing would suggest the attack is drawing closer. The second vision is very troubling, it suggests that her attacker and the theft is one of our students," Hex Queen said, very concerned.

"But which one?" David asked.

"That's the problem and I'm not sure how we could figure out who it is. A mystical blood test might work, but they would all have to be okay with it. Also, without a Fomorian to compare to, it would make any conclusions open to interpretation," Hex Queen thought out loud.

David decided to check on Circe and smiled when he saw her fast asleep. He told the two teachers and thanked them again for helping her. With Circe no longer tormented the two teachers headed off. The next morning Circe woke up to see her dad standing there.

"Please tell me, you haven't been there all night," she said.

"I haven't, I got up a few minutes ago. How are you feeling?"

"Not too bad, I slept well once those visions stopped. How were Professor Fargo and Hex Queen?"

He filled her in on what the teachers had said about her visions.

"And I was hoping today was going to be a good day," she said, not hearing what she was being told.

"Are you okay to go today, or would you prefer to stay at home?"

"I would prefer to continue my training."

She got ready though she was concerned about Professor Fargo and Hex Queen's interpretation of her visions being that one of her classmates was going to kill her. Still, she couldn't live in fear and it was hard to imagine any of her classmates killing her.

"Do you want me to pick you up afterwards?" Her dad asked.

"I'll see how I am," she said, she really didn't want him to worry.

Today was Hero Protocol class, so nothing stressful. As the class was in full swing, an alarm sounded.

"Klanga Klanga Klanga!"

"Is this a drill?" Hyperdrive asked his wife.

"That alarm is never used for a drill. Everyone, the city is under attack. Suit up and meet up outside the school," Elemental ordered.

For Circe and Alex changing was a matter of moments, so they were one of the first to arrive to see what was going on. Fomorians were attacking the city. Circe stood in fear, it was like her vision but she wasn't going to wake up in her bed, this was real. They were soon joined by the others along with the teachers. Professor Fargo addressed the group.

"The city is under attack from an ancient race called Fomorians. Don't let their strange looks fool you, these have threatened Hibernia for millennia. The pro heroes will deal with the Fomorians along with third year students. Second and first years and those on the hero training course, assist civilians and do not engage the enemy unless it is absolutely necessary. Everyone move out."

All the heroes warped back into the park and began to spread out. Circe was worried about her dad, but she couldn't let her worries affect her judgement.

"Hey, everything is going to be fine," Alex said, noticing her friend's worry.

"I don't know. This means my visions are coming true."

"But since we know about them, we can change them. Beside I'll keep you safe. I promise."

The two friends decided to stick together as they did their best to help the public. However, suddenly a giant swarm of Fomorians attacked them. The two friends tried their best to fend them off. It was clear to both of them that they were Circe was their main target. As they numbers kept growing, some of the Fomorians attempted to wrap metal about around Circe.

"They are trying to negate my powers!" Circe said, scared as she blasted away another Fomorian.

"We wouldn't let them, will we?" Alex said as she kept blasting some more.

"We need to get out of here and try and find more heroes," Circe said.

"I don't think they are going to let us."

Suddenly there was another blast but it wasn't from Alex or Circe. The blast came from Brendan.

"Looks like getting lost paid off," he said with a smile.

"Don't just stand there smiling. The Fomorian's are after Circe," Alex said.

"I know," and with a blast from his eyes, he hit not only the Fomorians but also Alex knocking her out.

"Alex!" Circe shouted before she could do anything else, a group of Fomorians piled on her and began wrapping iron bands around her.

"No, Stop," she said as she did everything to try and get them off.

"Don't worry I'll help," Brendan said as he fired another eye blast.

It was as the blast came towards her that Circe realised that her visions were trying to warn her that Brendan was going to betray… no, kill her. The blast hit her rendering her unconscious and along with the iron caused her to transform back to normal. He looked at the two helpless ladies and kicked Alex away.

"Sorry Alex, but I'm only interested in Circe," he said with an evil grin as he picked up the helpless Circe. "So beautiful, it's almost a shame to kill you."

Brendan along with some of the Fomorians headed off with Circe, while the other Fomorians continued to attack the city. A while later, Alex woke up to see Hex Queen casting a spell.

"This is just a healing spell. Don't worry," Hex Queen said.

"Circe! They have her," Alex said, horrified.

"What do you mean?" Hex Queen said, fearing the worst.

Alex quickly filled her in on what happened.

"This is bad, and the city is still full of Fomorians," Hex Queen said.

"They are probably a glorified distraction to stop us from finding Circe," Alex said, concerned for her friend's life.

Hex Queen immediately notified Professor Fargo and all the other heroes. Time was now of the essence but with an army of Fomorians still loose and no way of knowing where Circe as taken, it looked like all of Circe's visions would come true...

Chapter 6
Heroic Sacrifice

Circe's body twitched as she began to regain conscious. She tried to stretch but she couldn't. She tried to call out but she couldn't. She was restrained to a creepy pillar, her hands suspended above her head by a metal band, her legs were restrained together by another metal band and another was around her waist. They were all connected to the pillar, she tried to move but none of the restraints even budged. She tried to transform but a metal band was placed around her mouth preventing anything but some muffled noises to come through.

The metal bands were clearly made of iron as her powers weren't working. She was scared, her visions showed she was going to die and there was nothing she could do to stop it. No powers, no ability to scream, no idea where she was, no idea if her dad was safe, no idea if Alex was okay. All she knew was that Brendan betrayed them but why? Also, why she wasn't already dead? She might get her answers as a door opened in front of her and Brendan and some Fomorians entered the room.

"Looks like you are awake," he said with the Blade of Balor in his hand.

Circe struggled and made a number of muffled noises. Brendan just looked at her with a smile.

"Struggle as much as you want it isn't going to help, though you do look hot doing it."

Circe gave him a death glare. She maybe helpless but she wasn't going to give this pervert any pleasure.

"Still, it won't be too long now before the grand ceremony. At 3.32 p.m., the time Balor was killed by Lug, he will be resurrected."

3.32 a.m. was when she was found by her dad, was it a coincidence?

"Still, we might as well get you prepared," he said with a sadistic smile as he ripped her blouse open exposing her bra. "So, it's a matching set"

Circe tried to scream as she was exposed and realised what Brendan had done while she was unconscious, but the metal band around her mouth prevented her. She started cursing him, but again nothing but some muffled noises came out.

"You are so cute when you're angry. It is a shame I have to kill you. But in order for Balor to be reborn, I'm going to stab your pretty little body with his blade and the special blood from your heart will flow down your body and the pillar and into his heart buried under the circle beneath your feet," he said, using the blade to help explain what was going to happen.

She couldn't think of a way out, she was going to die at the hands of a pervert. She prayed that someone would find her. Unknown to her, people were trying to do just that. Alex along with Professor Fargo, Hex Queen and the others were trying to find her.

"I still can't believe Brendan betrayed us," Dermot said.

"None of us can and now Circe is in trouble," Siobhán said.

"Not just her, we all will be if this Balor guy comes back," Aoife said.

Professor Fargo was trying to think of where Circe could be. It wasn't easy with all the fighting as Elemental arrived.

"We are barely making a dent in these Fomorians. They just keep coming. I know this is a distraction, but even I would call this overkill for a villain," she said, giving a quick report.

"Thank you, Elizabeth, tell everyone to focus on keeping the civilians safe. Trying to defeat this army before Balor is revived seems to be pointless and will just weaken us."

"Understood," Elemental said as she then took off to re-join the battle.

"Where would they take her?" Alex said, fearing for Circe's safety.

"It would have to be wherever one of Balor's key parts was hidden. More than likely his heart. It would be somewhere in or near the city, but that information is sealed," Professor Fargo said.

"Where are the locations sealed? We need to unseal them," Alex said.

"Unfortunately, that information was sealed for the express purpose of preventing anyone from learning the locations of Balor's parts. Also, they are in the Royal Archives, so only the Royal Family could unseal them."

Upon hearing this. Alex flew up into the air and quickly made a phone call.

"Ciara, Yes I am fine, but Circe is in trouble. I need to know where Balor's Heart is located. Get my parents if you must, but hurry and message me the information the moment you get it. No wait, that will arouse suspicion, have mother, message Elemental."

Having made her urgent call. Alex quickly re-joined the others.

"What were you doing?" Patrick asked.

"I was hoping to get a better view, maybe get a clue or something. I promised I would keep her safe and I've failed."

"Hey, we'll find her. Don't lose hope," Siobhan said as Elemental returned.

"I have something," she said.

"What?" Professor Fargo.

"I just got a message from Queen Sarah. She said that Balor's Heart is located in Sunsport below Turgesius Tower," Elemental said.

"How did she know and how does she know your number?" Hex Queen asked.

"The message doesn't say but Queen Sarah and I have been friends for years."

"Wait, which one is Turgesius Tower?" Alex asked.

"The one near the Clock Tower," Professor Fargo said.

Alex quickly took off determined to save Circe.

"Damn it, Elizabeth go after her, we will catch up," Professor Fargo ordered.

Thanks to her armour, Alex was already at the tower. There was a large number of Fomorians around. Fighting them would waste time but sneaking around could also just be as consuming. However, she couldn't damage a historic building so she managed to sneak in. Below the building, time was running out.

"Since the defeat of Balor, the Fomorians have been trying to find a way to revive him. However, for years we didn't know how to resurrect him, but recently some of our druids discovered the way. All we were missing was a person with Divine blood and luckily for us, you happened to mention you had Divine powers," Brendan said, bragging to Circe.

"You see, I am a descendant of Bres, the half-Fomorian, half Tuatha De Danann god who sided with the Fomorians and enslaved the Tuatha De Danann. I was raised with the task as the rest of my family was to revive Balor. Today, that task ends with your death and the resurrection of Balor!"

With a massive thrust Brendan thrusted the Blade of Balor into Circe. Circe tried to scream as the blade sliced through her flesh and into her heart. Tears began to flow from her eyes as she could feel her life ending. She looked down as Brendan left the blade in the wound as blood began to emerge. However, to her surprise, it wasn't red but gold.

"The Blade reveals your blood's true form. Those crazy druids were right!" Brendan said, excited to see the gold blood.

His excitement was short lived as the door blew open and Alex emerged.

"Get away from her, you sick monster!" She said, fuming.

She fired off a number of blasts before Brendan could react hitting him and the Fomorians. With them stunned, she rushed to Circe and blasted her restraints. She caught Circe before she touched the ground.

"Circe, can you hear me?" She said, terrified to see what had happened to her friend.

"Don't let my...blood...touch... the cir...circle," Circe said weakly.

Alex was surprised to see gold blood coming from Circe but now wasn't the time. She knew she had to get Circe away but moving her could make things worse. A medical scan confirmed her worse fears, Circe was stabbed in the heart and was in critical condition. So far, the blade was the only thing keeping Circe from bleeding out completely. As she tried to decide Brendan fired an eye blast at her, knocking her and Circe over.

"You are not ruining this, Alex," Brendan said furiously as he made his way towards Circe firing blasts at Alex.

"Keep firing at me you idiot," Alex said, as another blast hit her.

Brendan didn't know that Alex's armour was adapting to the constant blasts and when he fired off one blast too many, her armour reflected it back at him. He cursed her name as she grabbed Circe and managed to see Elemental dealing with some of the Fomorians. However, Circe's condition got worse as during Brendan's blast bombardment, the Blade of Balor had been dislodged from her chest and she was bleeding more. Elemental quickly rushed to try and stop the bleeding.

"Circe, just hold on," she said as she also set up a defensive wall of earth between them and the Fomorians.

She used whatever first aid equipment she had in her belt. She knew though that unless Circe got proper treatment she would die. Thankfully, Professor Fargo, Hex Queen and the other heroes in training along with more heroes arrived. Hex Queen tried to perform a healing spell, but the wound was too deep.

"I can slow down the bleeding but that's the best I can do," Hex Queen said.

"Can she be moved?" Professor Fargo asked concerned for his student's safety.

"She can, but I would recommend someone fly her to the hospital. It's way too dangerous to go on the ground."

"I'll take her," Alex said, feeling guilty for Circe's injuries.

"Very well, but make sure she's comfortable and keep an eye on her vital signs," Hex Queen said, gently placing Circe into Alex's arms.

Alex gently took off, while the others decided to head inside Turgesius Tower and apprehend Brendan. Inside Brendan was furious.

"That witch, she'll pay. Balor be damned!"

He grabbed the Blade of Balor and licked whatever drops of Circe's blood were on the blade. The gold blood caused his body to transform. His whole body grew and contorted, his eyes merged into one, his hair grew wild as he smashed through the tower. He was no longer a human or even a Fomorian but closer to a god. Both heroes and Fomorians moved to avoid being crushed by the falling debris. Everyone looked in horror at the monstrous, giant form in front of them.

"What on Earth is that?" Dermot asked.

"Don't you recognise your old friend?" Brendan said.

"Brendan?"

"That's right but now I am your god!" Brendan shouted as he fired a gigantic eye blast.

The blast tore through the city, between the Fomorians and now the laser blasting giant, panic was everywhere. The heroes and emergency services did everything they could to help the civilians.

"Lizzie, any ideas on how we fight that?" Hyperdrive asked his wife.

"Giants aren't exactly my speciality," Elemental replied.

"What can take that down?" Patrick asked scared.

"Don't panic we'll come up with a plan. For now, try to prevent him from destroying the city," Hex Queen said before turning to Professor Fargo. "This army was bad enough but now we have this to deal with. We can't fight Brendan and an army at the same time."

"Maybe we need to level the playing field," Professor Fargo said, grabbing his cane and seemingly ready to channel dark energy through it.

"No!" Hex Queen said, grabbing the cane.

"Vivian, it could help us."

"And ruin you, you... we have done so much together. You can't throw it away even to help others. You only get one second chance, Fargo," Hex Queen said with tears in her eyes.

"You're right I'm sorry. It's just with one student near death and another being a traitor, I feel like I have failed as an educator."

"You are a wonderful educator and don't lose faith. Now how do we deal with this."

"Well, if we defeat Brendan, then the Fomorians will also be defeated. However, we don't know how powerful he is. Also, Vivian, thank you," Professor Fargo said.

"Terry, wait!"

Professor Fargo and Hex Queen looked to see Elemental calling out to her husband. Hyperdrive clearly wasn't going to wait around and decided to try and attack Brendan

159

"Giants may not be my speciality but I know that nothing can survive a decapitation," he thought to himself as he readied to cut through Brendan's neck from behind.

He made his attack but his energy sword's blade broke as he struck the back of Brendan's neck. Brendan turned towards Hyperdrive and swatted him with his arm. Hyperdrive crashed into the ground.

"TERRY!" Elemental quickly flew to where her husband had landed. "TERRY! CAN YOU HEAR ME?!"

"Ugh, Stop shouting, I can hear you, the armour took the impact, though it's totalled," Hyperdrive said as he got up and his armour broke around him.

Elemental embraced her husband just happy he was alright. Meanwhile Brendan laughed.

"Fools, I am a god, only a being of equal divine might could beat me," he said as he fired out another blast.

"So, how many gods do we have?" PainTrain said, having punched his way through.

"You're not supposed to ask that," Elemental said.

"Currently, the only hero in Sunsport with Divine powers... is Circe," Professor Fargo said.

"He could be bluffing. We might not need Divine powers to defeat him," Elemental said.

"Elizabeth's right. Villains love to brag and boast," Hex Queen said.

"Even so we better request any and all Divine power types to come here before it is too late," Professor Fargo said.

"Wouldn't that take hours?" Dermot asked.

"Not quite, the country does have teleporters in most hero institutions. The school included."

"You mean the school he's starting to head towards," Aoife said, pointing to Brendan being to head towards the park.

"What about the whole other realm thing? Shouldn't that keep the school safe?" Siobhán asked.

"He would have access since he was a student," Patrick said, "assuming he can shrink back down."

"We can't risk it. We have to stop him before he reaches the park," Professor Fargo said as everything spring into action.

Meanwhile Alex was taking the injured Circe to the hospital but neither could ignore what was happening.

"It's… all my… fault," Circe weakly said.

"It's not your fault," Alex said, trying to comfort Circe.

"Alex… I don't…want to die…with that on…my conscience."

"You aren't going to die. You are going to be fine."

"Even in… that armour, I can see…that… you're lying. My heart hurts," Circe said weakly and clearly in pain.

"Elemental and Hex Queen could only heal the opening to prevent you from bleeding out, but they couldn't heal the actual damage to your heart. Just don't look back, we'll be at the hospital in no time," Alex said briefly retracting her faceplate to reveal that she was crying but only in one eye.

Circe couldn't help looking back and see Brendan on a rampage. She broke down in tears.

"People are going… to die and it's my… fault."

"People aren't going to die and it's my fault. I didn't keep you safe like I promised," Alex said as she then got an update about what was going on. "Everything's going to be fine, more heroes are coming."

"Which ones…"

"They aren't saying but it looks like some heavy hitters apparently Brendan thinks he's a god and that only a god can beat him…" Alex realised she shouldn't have said that.

"I… have to stop him…"

"Don't even think about it. You are in a critical condition. Even if you could stop him, transforming could kill you."

"Athrú"

She couldn't ignore it. She had to do something. If she had the power to stop Brendan then she would. The transformation was more painful as it seemed her body was forcing itself to heal. Alex looked to see Circe transformed and seemingly in better health.

"Are you insane? That could have killed you! "Alex said furiously.

"Scan me, Please," Circe said.

"You have stopped bleeding and there seems to be no damage on your heart. However, there is no guarantee, you will remain healed if you transform back or for how long you will stay transformed. Please, let me take you to the hospital."

"Alex, my hometown is being destroyed thanks to my blood. I can't just lay in a bed knowing that people could be dying. You promised to keep me safe, but I can't ignore what's happening."

"Fine, but I'm coming with you," Alex said reluctantly.

As the two friends headed back towards the battle. The battle was raging. Elemental dosed Brendan with water before letting Patrick fire as much electricity as he could. Other heroes launched similar combined assaults.

"So far we are slowing him down but that's about it," Elemental said.

"That gives more heroes the chance to help us," Professor Fargo said.

"Still there has to be something that can stop him," Hex Queen stated as she prepared herself.

She gestured her arms and cast a spell.

"I call upon beloved Hecate, goddess of Witchcraft. Empower your child with powers from time immortal and fuel my spirit with your might. One Thousand Hex Spheres!"

Brendan was hit by a thousand energy bombs. He screamed in pain, but while the explosions injured him it wasn't enough. Hex Queen collapsed from using the spell.

"That was amazing!" Siobhán said, "You actually hurt him."

"Only because I channelled a god's power through me," Hex Queen said, clearly weakened.

"You did great Vivian, now rest," Professor Fargo said.

"I really wish I could try again, but…" Hex Queen said.

"What's wrong?" Siobhan asked.

"Using certain magic comes with a cost, especially channelling a deity. She just shortened her life," Professor Fargo said.

"Oh no."

"Relax it was just a few months. There's still plenty of life left in me."

"I wouldn't be so sure," Brendan said, still sore from Hex Queen's attack.

He decided to squash them all like bugs, however a number of fuchsia coloured energy blasts hurt him and knocked him off balance, causing him to crash.

"Please tell me, he didn't fall on anyone," Circe said to Alex concerned.

"Well, you ruined your awesome entrance by asking that, but he didn't squash anyone," Alex said, quickly scanning.

Hearing the news made Circe feel relieved. The two touched down beside Professor Fargo and the others. They were shocked to see Circe back.

"What are you doing here? You should be at the hospital," Professor Fargo said, clearly not pleased.

"I couldn't stand by while this monster was destroying the city thanks to my blood," Circe said.

"He's bleeding," Aoife said, noticing Brendan's wounds has he got up.

"So, you returned just to die. You must be a bimbo," he said, mocking and threatening Circe.

Circe fired other series of blasts, which caused even more pain.

"It's not enough, he's too big," Elemental said.

"Then Circe will have to concentrate all of her energy into one blast," Hex Queen said.

"Can she do that?" PainTrain asked, "Because that's a lot to ask of one lady."

"She'll have to if we are to stand a chance. Vivian, help Circe channel her powers," Professor Fargo said.

"Shouldn't you? You're her mentor."

"I should, but you are the better teacher, besides, you can't fight at the moment and we need everyone to keep Brendan's attention away for Circe."

Professor Fargo led everyone to attack Brendan with everything they got. While Hex Queen to quickly train Circe.

"You already know, how to charge a blast, but you will need to charge everything you have into one blast. So, first thing first," Hex Queen said as she created a magical barrier.

Circe took a deep breath and began to concentrate. Hex Queen told her how to hold on to the power she was generating. Hex Queen was concerned that given her injuries though seemingly healed, Circe might not be strong enough to do what was asked of her. Meanwhile the other heroes tried to give Circe as much time as she needed.

"Hey, blockhead, say cheese!" Aoife said, generating a blinding light.

"Aggh! My eyes!"

While he was blinded. Declan and some other super-fast heroes wrapped cables around Brendan's legs. Dermot, PainTrain and some other heroes then pulled the cables, causing him to fall. Elemental then dowsed him in water, then Siobhan summoned a lightning storm to strike him, while Patrick fired electricity at him. Other heroes fired whatever type of attacks they had, all aiming for the injures that both Hex Queen and Circe had caused. Alex was trying to focus on the task at hand, but her thoughts were of Circe and fearing she was pushing herself too far. Professor Fargo noticed Alex's concern even through her helmet.

"It might be best if you stay with Circe," he said.

"But I should be here with everyone else."

"Where a hero should be in a crisis, should depend on where they can best help people. I believe that you will do more good with Circe."

"Okay," Alex said, heading towards Circe and Hex Queen.

Brendan started waving his arms and firing random blasts to stop the heroes. Despite their best efforts he managed to get back on his feet and remove the cables. He then stomped on the ground causing a miniature earthquake, which caused the heroes to lose their footing. It also affected Circe and Hex Queen, but Alex managed to catch Circe before she lost her concentration.

"Alex?"

"It's okay, I'm here. Just keep doing what you're doing."

"Excellent timing. We are nearly ready," Hex Queen said, getting back on her feet.

With Alex supporting her, Circe felt even more strength within her. Her power grew and grew. Soon she had mustered all she had. Her hands were now glowing at their brightest. She was ready. She aimed at Brendan and thinking of everyone she wanted to protect, she fired. A giant energy blast of fuchsia energy and engulfed Brendan. Brendan screamed as the blast vaporised him and then where there was a giant god, there was nothing.

"You did it!" Alex said before noticing Circe transforming back and making a small whimper.

Circe's injuries had reopened, she was struggling to stay conscious. Hex Queen did her best to heal her before Alex rushed her to the hospital. During the flight Circe was getting weaker.

"Circe, By my Royal Command, I order you not to die!" Alex proclaimed as Circe lost consciousness.

"Circe?"

Alex looked in horror.

"CIRCE!"

Chapter 7
It's Over, Finished...

Brendan Ross, the self-proclaimed Fomorian God had been defeated, but the victory wasn't without cost. Heroes and civilians had been injured in his rampage following the failed resurrection of Balor. In one room of Sunsport Hospital, the woman... no, Hero who stopped him and saved so many lives now lay fighting for her own life after nearly been sacrificed. David Goodwin sat beside his daughter, hoping and praying that she would recover.

"Please don't take my Circe," he prayed or begged to any deity that might be listening.

Her condition was grim. Being stabbed in the heart, then magically transforming to help battle Brendan and then releasing so much magical energy it destroyed a giant, put so much strain on an already damaged and weaken body. It was a miracle she was even alive when she reached the hospital.

It seemed like ages when he heard a small moan coming from Circe. He rushed over to see her open her eyes and he got a shock.

"Dad..." she said weakly.

"Take it easy, you've been to a lot," he said, trying to stop her getting up.

"Brendan…"

"You stopped him, you saved so many people. I'm so proud of you."

"That's good to hear," she said, already sounding stronger, but then noticed her dad was looking at her strangely. "What's wrong?"

"Your eyes, they're still Fuchsia!"

"Seriously? Didn't I transform back after I fired off that blast?"

"You did!"

"Is this a permanent change?" Circe said, shocked when she managed to see her eyes in a mirror.

"I don't know, and you should not be putting yourself under any more strain," David said, trying to calm his daughter down.

"Yeah, you're right," Circe said, taking a deep breath.

"I'm going to get a doctor and let them know you are awake," he said as he left the room.

It didn't take David too long to get a doctor. The doctor did an examination of Circe and was surprised by the results.

"Well Ms Goodwin, if it wasn't for the fact that I was the one who operated on you, I would never have known that you were stabbed in the heart," The doctor said with a smile on their face.

"What do you mean?" David asked confused.

"I have checked and there is no wound. Apart from the fact she is still a little weak and her change in eye colour, she's healthy," The Doctor said.

"Well, that's good to hear," Circe said, happy to hear that she was on the mend.

"Still, she should be resting. So, I would limit visitors," The doctor said.

"Okay doctor, thank you," David said as the doctor left.

He then turned to his daughter and hugged her.

"I was so scared I lost you," he said.

"I'm sorry for scaring you," she said.

David then showed Circe a photo.

"What's all this?" She was shocked to see what looked like the hallway of the castle filled with flowers, cards and gifts.

"That's all the thank you and get well soon cards you have gotten from the public."

"That's insane! I can believe people would do that for me!"

"Circe, you saved all their lives, you shouldn't be surprised that they want you to be okay and want to thank you."

"Yeah, it's just I've never seen that much in my life."

As the days past, Circe was released for the hospital and was busy looking through all the cards, flowers and gifts. She decided to send everyone a thank you card back and due to the cost, she was making her own. They weren't going to be fancy, but they would have a more distinctive touch. As she took a break, her phone rang, she checked and saw it was Alex.

"Hi Alex!" she said excited.

"Hey, I heard you were home, and I wanted to see how you were." Alex said excitedly over the phone.

"Well, I got a full bill of health and I'm currently trying to thank everyone for all their gifts and cards. I was surprised you didn't visit me, while I was in the hospital."

"Great to hear. I wanted to visit, but sadly other things kept getting in the way."

"Actually, can we meet up? I want to talk to you about something."

"Sure, I'm free tomorrow. Where do you want to meet?"

"Could you meet me at my house? What I want to say is quite private."

"Okay, sure." Alex said, a bit confused.

The two talked for a bit longer and Circe went back to making her cards.

The next day, Alex headed from Sunsport's train station to St. Declan's castle. She looked over to see the City still recovering from Brendan's attack. The Royal Family had promised to rebuild Sunsport to its former glory as soon as possible and it was clear they were keeping their promise. While she and Circe were friends since they first met all those weeks ago, she had never been to her house. She walked up the hill and arrived at the front door. She rang the doorbell and Circe quickly answered.

"You made it, this way," she said, excited.

"Wait, your eyes!" Alex said, shocked to see Circe had fuchsia eyes.

"Yeah, I'm not too sure how it happened. I emailed Professor Fargo about it and while he's looking into it; he believes it could be that this is actually my natural eye colour, and my green eyes were magically coloured."

"I see...So, you actually live her?" Alex said, looking around.

"This is actually the school, we live here," Circe said as she led Alex to the clock that was the door to her family's apartment.

"Cool a secret passage," Alex said as the two walked down the passageway. "Are these all photos of you and your dad?" She said, also noticing the photos that lined the passageway.

"Pretty much, there are some of my grandparents, but yeah they are all family photos."

They arrived in the main apartment and Alex was surprised at how small it was. Circe got took drinks out of the fridge and some homemade cake and took Alex to her room.

"Your dad not around?"

"No, he's getting some things for the school. Besides, I thought it would be better for us to talk alone."

"About what?"

"Remember when I saved you from the Dearg Due, you said you wanted to repay me."

"Yeah, and you said it was okay."

"Well, there is something you can do…"

"What?"

"I want you to be honest with me Alex, or as you allowed me to call you… Edelgard."

Alex's eye widened by the reveal.

"You know…" she said, shocked.

"I'm guessing that I'm right then."

Alex let out a huge sigh and pressed some hidden buttons on her bracelets. Her hair changed from blonde to white and her eyes changed from brown to a piercing blue. Standing in front of Circe was not her friend Alex but Edelgard, Princess of Hibernia.

"You are correct, Circe. I am really Princess Edelgard" she said in a more regal tone.

"You could have just denied it."

"You wanted me to be honest, and I wanted to tell you."

"I'm suspecting that this whole secret, secret identity is to protect yourself and your family as I'm sure that some members of the public would have a fit if they knew the heir to the throne was risking her life as a hero."

"Again, you are very perspective. Also, I would prefer to keep it a secret."

"Don't worry your secret is safe, though would it be okay to tell my dad?"

"As long as he understands the secrecy, I have no problems. I would hate for your family to have secrets from each other. Still, I have to know; how did you know my secret?"

"You do remember when me first met? I happened to mention your white hair despite you had blonde hair. At first, I thought it was something wrong with my eyes, but when I learned I could see hidden objects, I suspected that you were trying to hide your white hair. There was the incident with the Guardsmen, which I'm still not sure how you did that, but it was when we were invited to the Castle that I knew.

First of all, there was the fact that the Royal Residence knew my email, I assumed that Professor Fargo might have given it to them, which he could have been I'm sure he would have asked my permission. However, when The King happened to mention I had Divine powers, I knew something was up. There was only one way he would have known and that was if someone had told him It wouldn't have been Professor Fargo as he said that a person's origin was personal. So, the only way he would have known is if someone, like his daughter told him."

"That I have to apologise for. I did not expect my father to ever mention your origin, especially in front of you," Edelgard said, clearly embarrassed.

"Then there was the way you acted after you allowed me to call you by your name and not a title. You sounded more like Alex than Edelgard."

"I am human after all. Sometimes my emotions do get the best of me," Edelgard said, again clearly embarrassed.

"Oh, and before I lost consciousness, I heard you say, 'By my Royal Command, I order you not to die!'"

"I panicked. I didn't want you to die, so it was the only thing I could think off. No-one can disobey a Royal Command. I'm only glad no-one else heard it."

"Also, I noticed that both Alex and Edelgard only wipe away tears from one eye and never the eye that is covered by their hair."

"That's because that eye does not work," Edelgard said, lifting her hair revealing a whited-out eye with some scarring around it. "When I was a baby, some assassins managed to access my bedroom and attempted to kill me and my mother with a bomb under my crib. My mother managed to shield me from most of the blast, though her arm was damaged and some of the shrapnel struck my eye. I cannot see through it, nor does it cry."

"I'm so sorry and is that also why you panicked when that bomb went off?"

"Indeed, I have a fear of explosions. My armour dulls the noise, and I am not a fan of fireworks. I should explain that, that bomb was a fake. My parents thought the whole scheme up so you would have to be indebted to me as Edelgard, so I could pay you back. I was completely against it, but it can be hard to argue with my parents sometimes."

"Seriously, that was all a scam just so I would have to accept you being indebted to me," Circe said, annoyed.

"I am terribly sorry. When you saved my life as Alex, I was honour bound as a Princess to repay you and since you would not accept being indebted to Alex. My parents made it so you would have to save Edelgard's life."

"So, which is the real you? Since Alex and Edelgard don't act the same."

"They are both the real me. Most of the time, I am Princess Edelgard, heir to the throne, who is polite and acts as she has been taught to behave as a Princess. The other time, I am Alex, just an intelligent teenager. But what matters is that I am in love with you, Circe."

"Wait, what did you say?" Circe was taken aback by the sudden love declaration.

"I am in love with you, but I understand if you do not feel the same way," Edelgard said.

She wondered if she should have admitted her feelings. Revealing her true identity was a big reveal, to then drop a love declaration on top of that, might have been going a bit too far. However, her fears were elevated when Circe kissed her on the lips.

"I think that answered how I feel," Circe said with a smile.

"I do not know, you better kiss me again, just to make sure," Edelgard said with a smile as the two kissed again.

"I can't believe I'm kissing a princess," Circe said.

"I cannot believe you are kissing me."

"So, are we officially an item now?" Circe asked.

"I would very much like that. Are you comfortable with being the Princess's girlfriend? It would be in the spotlight more and certain things would be expected of you," Edelgard said.

"If it means I can be with you then I have no problems," Circe said with a s reassuring smile.

The two kissed again when David entered the room.

"Circe, are you in here? I called but you didn't answer"

"DAD! It... It's not what it looks like," Circe said, startled and embarrassed.

"So, you are not kissing... the Princess..." David said, shocked at seeing Princess Edelgard in his daughter's room. He quickly bowed.

"Please, I am a guest in your home. There is no need for protocol," Edelgard said.

"Circe, why is the Princess in your room? I thought you were meeting Alex today to talk about something?"

"Well," Circe looked at Edelgard who nodded. "Edelgard is also Alex."

Circe quickly explained to her father about Edelgard's dual identity and the need to keep it a secret.

"Don't worry your secret is safe with me. Now about the other matter of you kissing the Princess," David said to Circe.

"Ehh..." Circe said, embarrassed and trying to think of how to explain it to her dad.

"Circe, it's fine."

"Thanks Dad," Circe said, happy that her dad was okay with her dating Edelgard.

"I just hope my father will be as understanding," Edelgard said.

"Why?" Circe asked concerned.

"My father is… a bit of a traditionalist. I am not sure that he has fully accepted that the heir to the throne is a lesbian. He is not a homophobe or anything like that, he is just concerned about the future of the royal lineage," Edelgard said, trying to explain as best as she could.

"I'm sure he'll be fine with it," Circe said with a reassuring smile.

Edelgard stayed for a while longer, briefing both Goodwins on some of the things that will be expected of Circe if her family accepted the two dating. Soon she had to return to Kingdom City, she became Alex once again and headed off.

"So, you saved the country and now are dating the Princess," David said with a smile.

"I can hardly believe it myself, and you are okay with me dating Edelgard?"

"Yes, though I'm still getting use to you calling her on a first name basis. Still how are you going with all those cards?"

"I have most of them done, though how to get them to everyone is another thing. The postage is going to be expensive."

"We'll figure something out."

Later that day, Circe got a call from Edelgard.

"Is everything okay?" Circe asked a bit concerned

"I thought I would notify would that my parents are planning a huge celebration in your honour. You will be getting an email probably tomorrow underlining all the details. As the guest of honour and my girlfriend, attendance is mandatory."

"So, have you talked to your parents about us dating? Especially as you just referred to me as your girlfriend."

"Well, I have not told them yet." Edelgard said nervously over the phone.

"Edelgard!" Circe was shocked, she thought given how sudden her love confession was, that Edelgard would have told her parents as soon as possible.

"To be honest, I was hoping that you could be there with me, when I do tell them."

"Sure, when do you want to tell them?"

"Maybe when you get the email you could come up the day after and then we can tell them. Also, it would allow us to answer any questions you might have."

"Okay, I'll make sure my dad is okay with it and I will hopefully see you soon."

Sure enough, the Goodwins were heading once again to Kingdom City and the Castle. It wasn't like last time, now Circe and Edelgard were dating (well, hopefully). Circe was checking the printout of email about the event in her honour, along with another sheet of paper she had written some notes on.

"Do you think they will be okay with some of the ideas?" She said, once again checking her notes.

"I think the whole thing is a great idea. I'm sure they'll love them."

"Do you think they will be okay with me dating Edelgard?"

"I have no problem, so they shouldn't either."

"I hope so."

The arrived at the Castle and were greeted by Edelgard. Since it wasn't a formal event, she was wearing blue jacket, white shirt and black trousers and boots all with gold trim and a gold belt. Even it was causal wear for her, it looked extremely fancy in Circe's eyes.

"My parents are waiting in the living room," Edelgard said as she led the Goodwins around.

The three arrived at a large set of doors, which a member of the Castle's staff opened for the Princess and her guests. The Goodwins bowed to the King and Queen and everyone sat down, with the king and Queen on one large Sofa, Edelgard and Circe on another sofa and David on another. The Goodwins felt almost out of place on the large regal sofas.

"So, Circe, what do you think of our plans for the celebrations?" King Brian said.

"Father before we talk about that, there is something that I want to talk to you about. I invited Circe and her father here, because of what I am about to say. Father, Mother, I am in love with Circe, and I wish to have your blessing in pursuing a relationship with her," Edelgard said, holding or pretty much squeezing Circe's hand, despite her regal tone, Circe knew she was nervous.

The King and Queen looked at each other. The two started whispering to each other, before looking at their daughter with a smile on each of their faces.

"You have both mine and your mother's blessing to date Circe," King Brian said.

Both ladies smiled at each other and quickly kissed each other, almost forgetting that their parents were in the room. They quickly regained their composures as a Princess and her guest would behave.

"I am correct in saying that you have no objection to Circe dating our Edelgard," Queen Sarah asked David.

"None, Your Majesty," David replied.

"Father, you are okay with me dating Circe?" Edelgard said, still surprised that her dad was okay with her dating.

"I would not be a good father if I got in the way of my daughter's happiness."

"What about the royal bloodline? Aren't you afraid that I will not be able to produce an heir?"

"That is something we can all deal with, in the future. Just focus on your happiness and your girlfriend. However, there is a problem about your relationship that has to dealt with now."

"You just gave your blessing," Edelgard said, annoyed that her father seemed to be changing his mind.

"It is your dual identity. You have already informed your mother and I that Circe and her father know that you and Alex are the same. However, Circe cannot date both Alex and Edelgard. You both have to decide which of your identities Circe will date in public. I don't expect you to decide right away, but you should decide before you make your relationship public."

"We had not actually thought of that, but we will settle on it before the celebrations," Edelgard said.

Speaking of which, we were going to discuss the plans for the celebrations. So, Circe what do you think?" Queen Sarah said.

"To be honest… "Circe said, hesitating.

"Please, do not be nervous. We would prefer you to be honest about any reservations, rather than for you hide any problems due to the fear of criticising the Royal Family," Queen Sarah said.

"It's just, I'm not keen on the idea of it being all about me," Circe said, "I understand, you want to thank me for defeating Brendan or whatever he became and while I did eventually vaporise him. I wasn't the only hero there."

"Yeah, but you said it yourself that you were the only one who could stop him," Edelgard said.

"Maybe, but if you hadn't saved me from being sacrificed, I wouldn't be here. Also, all the heroes, even our classmates helped, some even got injured. So, I was thinking why not make it a celebration to all heroes. Also, with Sunsport still recovering it would really help the public. I have a couple of ideas, though I have never planned something like this."

She handed Edelgard her ideas. Edelgard looked at them herself, before handing the sheet to her parents. Circe was now thinking she should have presented them better, especially if the King and Queen were going to read them. The Royal couple both read the ideas and again whispered to each other, which made Circe nervous.

"We both think it is a wonderful idea," King Brian said as Circe breathed a sigh of relief. "Of course, we will need to fine tune your plans if that is alright with you."

"Of course," said Circe.

"Just do not think you are getting out of being the Guest of Honour," Edelgard stated with a smile.

"I was sort of hoping it would," Circe said with a nervous smile.

"Nonsense, you saved the Kingdom and besides, you are now my girlfriend. Which is still something we need to discuss. Father, Mother, may Circe and I be excused?"

"You are both excused," King Brian said as Circe and Edelgard left the room.

"Now that the lovebirds are away, there is something I was hoping you could help me with?" David said.

"What do you need?" Queen Sarah asked.

"Circe mentioned a tapestry room, she saw last time she was here. If it is possible, I would like to see it."

"Of course, please follow us," Queen Sarah said as she and her husband led David to the tapestry room.

Inside the room, David was amazed by all the tapestries. He listened to the Royal Couple as the described each of the tapestries in detail. It was strange having the rulers of his country act as tour guides, but it was also a rare experience. After they had finished with the explanations. David looked at the tapestry that Circe had talked about after their first visit here He looked at the character of Ériu very carefully.

"Is everything okay?" King Brian asked, noticing David staring at the tapestry.

"It's just the Goddess Ériu now has the same eye colour as Circe and given one of Circe's powers is, though limited, precognition, she was thinking that her powers might have some connection to her. I just wanted to see the tapestry for myself, and I can see where she is coming from."

"Maybe, there is more to it than that," Queen Sarah said.

"What do you mean, Your Majesty?"

"I mean given she has Divine powers and the similarities between the Goddess Ériu and Circe, maybe Circe is actually Divine. Forgive me, but Edelgard did mention to us that you nor Circe know anything about her true parentage; did it not occur to you that maybe Circe's parents could be someone like a God or a Goddess?"

"It didn't, to be honest, Circe said she has no interest in finding her biological parents."

"Of course, we understand."

While their parents were looking at Circe's past. Circe and Edelgard were in Edelgard's room, ready to discuss their future.

"Wow! What a view! You can see the river," Circe said, looking out the main window.

"Indeed, it is a splendid view to look at each morning. Of course, my father is right, we have to decide which of my identities you will be dating in public," Edelgard said, sitting on her bed as Circe joined her.

"So, while I'm dating you, I can publicly only date you or Alex?"

"Exactly, Alex would be easier for you. People already know we are friends, so it could be seen as a progression of our relationship. It would also allow you to avoid a lot of the public spotlight you would get by dating a Princess. However, for me, it would require actually creating more of Alex's life, including a family and home. If you decide to date Edelgard, there is all the publicity along with various Royal protocol you will be expected to follow as my girlfriend. Also, it would be harder for us to actually meet in public. Though it would be more truthfully, if a bit harder to explain due to the fact of my dual identity."

"This is a difficult decision. Which would you prefer?" Circe said, scratching her head.

"Personally, I would prefer you to date me as Edelgard. I want to show the whole country, no, the entire world the woman I am in love with. However, that would be selfish, the pressure that would be put on you would be immense."

"So, if I go with Alex, you will need to flesh out Alex more putting more pressure on you, especially if people start digging around Alex's background. If I go with Edelgard, the pressure will be on me with all the media exposure," Circe said, thinking aloud.

"Exactly."

"Well, if that's the case I know who I want to date," Circe said with a smile.

"Technically, you are dating me, no matter the identity. Still, if you have reached a decision, I would very much like to hear it."

"I want to date you Edelgard," Circe said, kissing her.

"Are you sure? I mean the media..." Edelgard said, a bit surprised but relieved.

"The media will be all over me, given I saved the Kingdom and what will happen when I'm your guest of honour at the celebrations."

"Are you sure?"

"You already asked me that and I'm fine with it. Beside you could easily order them to back off if necessary."

"That would be an abuse of my royal power, but it could be possible," Edelgard said, half-joking. "Still, if you are certain..."

"I'm certain."

"Then I can do this," Edelgard said with delight as she removed the ring, she always wore on her right ring finger and turned it around before putting it back on.

"Is that a Claddagh Ring?" Circe asked, noticing what Edelgard had just done.

"It is, in fact it is my royal Claddagh Ring which contains my royal seal. That's how I got those Guardsmen to leave us alone. I was given it when I reached thirteen by my parents. It is used to show my relationship status. Since, you have captured my heart, the heart is now pointing towards me," Edelgard said, showing Circe her ring.

"And because it is still on your right hand, it only means you are in a relationship," Circe said, remembering what she was told about the Claddagh Ring.

"Exactly, of course, now that I have done this, when I appear in public, people will notice and start asking questions. In fact, I have a public engagement tomorrow. There is a new art gallery opening tomorrow and I have been asked to official open it."

"So, what will you say if people do ask?"

"I will only state that I am in a relationship, but I will not be discussing anything until the hero celebrations. If it is okay with you, I would love to introduce you as my girlfriend then."

"I see no problem with that. First we have to plan this whole celebration first."

"Of course, and you will be constantly informed as it was your idea. Oh, before I forget..." Edelgard said as she quickly took out a small box from her jacket's pocket and handed it to Circe.

"What's this?"

"Open it."

Circe opened the small box to see a silver Claddagh Ring.

"Is this?"

"It is yours, put it on."

"Aren't these very expensive?"

"Not for love."

Circe wasn't going to argue, she placed the ring with its heart pointing inwards on to her right ring finger.

"I hope I have put it on right." She said, showing it to Edelgard.

"It's perfect and I hope you do not mind that mine is gold while your ring is silver."

"I don't mind, though I'm sure this is the most expensive thing I own."

The two young lovers talked some more when there was a knock on the door.

"You may enter!" Edelgard said with full regal authority as a member of the staff entered.

"Sorry to interrupt Your Highness, but His Majesty wants to inform you that Ms Goodwin will have to be leaving soon and your and Ms Goodwin's presence is requited in the main hall."

"Very well, we will be there momentarily," Edelgard said as the staff member bowed and left. "I would love for you to stay over."

"Maybe we can arrange something later. Still, we better not keep your parents waiting."

The two arrived in the main hall where their parents were waiting.

"I see you two have made your choice," Queen Sarah said, noticing both ladies' Claddagh rings.

"Indeed, we have Mother. Circe has decided to date me as myself," Edelgard announced with delight.

"And Circe, you are okay with what dating Edelgard may entail?" King Brian asked.

"I understand," Circe said reassuringly.

"I already asked her twice Father," Edelgard stated.

"Just making sure. David, are you okay with Circe publicly dating Edelgard?"

"I told her I would support any decision she made, and I stand by that."

"So, Edelgard, you have that Art Gallery opening tomorrow, how are you going to explain your ring?" Queen Sarah asked.

"I will inform anyone who notices my ring, that I have recently fallen for someone, and I will not be revealing any details until we are both ready to make our relationship public. That will be revealed during the hero celebrations," Edelgard explained.

"Let us hope they will accept that," King Brian said.

"Well, that will be all they will be getting until the celebrations," Edelgard said confidently.

"We better be heading home," Brian said to Circe.

"Yeah, but before we go," Circe said as she gave Edelgard a huge kiss goodbye.

"Goodbye Your Majesties, your Highness!" David said as he and Circe both bowed.

On the way home, Circe was marvelling her new ring.

"So, what does Princess Circe think of officially dating Princess Edelgard?" Her dad said jokingly.

"I'm not a Princess," Circe said, slightly embarrassed.

"You are to me, and you haven't answered my question."

"I'm excited, though I am a bit nervous of what the reaction will be when Edelgard makes it public. I'm also nervous of anything happening to this ring."

"I still can't believe she just gave it to you."

"Well, it is a symbol of our love, a symbol which is the most expensive thing I own, which makes me even more nervous about anything happening to it. So, did you go on the tour like I suggested?"

"I did and I saw the tapestry you mentioned, and Queen Sarah had an interesting theory."

"A theory about what?"

"Well, after seeing the tapestry and your new eye colour, the Queen suggested that instead of a God giving you Divine powers, you might actually be one."

"So, one or both of my biological parents could be a God. That's sounds like something from a Greek myth" Circe said, surprised.

"Says the girl whose name came from a book of Greek Myths that was left with her when she was a baby."

"You don't think it could be true, do you?"

"Like I said, it is only a theory the Queen thought of. Unless you have changed your mind and want to find out more about your biological parents?"

"I am still happy with knowing that you are my Dad. I don't need any other information about my parentage. As you said, it is just a theory," Circe said sincerely.

David decided to drop the subject. It was her decision, and he would support it.

"So, are you going to wear your new ring all the time?" He asked.

"Of course, Edelgard gave it to me as a symbol of our love. Why would I remove it?"

"While the Princess can deflect any questions that might arise from her ring. You never even had a Claddagh Ring until today. How are you going to explain that until the celebrations?"

"I hadn't thought about that. I could say it's an heirloom I was given."

"and the fact it is saying you are in a relationship?"

"Emm…"

"Relax, I'm just messing with you," David said. "Of course, You should wear it."

The next day, Circe had finally finished with all the Thank You cards. She looked at the pile of cards and then looked at her new ring.

"I'm a very lucky woman," she thought to herself.

"So, you are finally finished," David said as he entered with some groceries.

"Yeah, now we just have to find a way of handing them out," she said as she helped put away the groceries.

"Maybe your girlfriend could help."

"I'm not going to ask her for money!" Circe said, shocked at her Dad's suggestion.

"I'm just joking. Still, she might have some ideas. Speaking of which, didn't she have a gallery opening today?"

"She did, I wonder how she got on?"

"Well, the news should be on now, so let's see if there is any mention."

They went into the sitting room and turn on the T.V.

"Today's top story, Princess Edelgard is in a relationship," The newscaster said, causing both Goodwins to look at each other dumbfounded. The newscaster continued to report.

"The Princess was opening a new art gallery in Kingdom City when some of the public noticed that the Princess's Royal Claddagh ring had changed to point inwards, symbolising she was in a relationship. The Princess would not go into details, only to confirm she was in a relationship. Her Highness said she wanted to enjoy her new relationship in private for the time being, but she will reveal more in due time.

"Her Highness said there will be an official statement about her change in status by the end of the day. Her Highness did reveal that there are plans to thank all the heroes who helped stop the attack of the Fomorian Brendan Ross in Sunsport. She wouldn't go into further details as the event is still being planned, but she did confirm that Circe Goodwin, the young hero who defeated Brendan Ross will be the Guest of Honour."

"Looks like you are the top story," David said with a smile.

"I wasn't expecting that our relationship to be the thing everyone would be talking about," Circe said, still getting over the shock.

"You even got mentioned."

"Thankfully only as the celebration's Guest of Honour."

Suddenly Circe's phone rang.

"It's Edelgard."

"Then you better answer it."

"Hello, Edelgard."

"Hello, Love of my life. I trust you have seen the news."

"My Dad and I were just watching it. I can't believe it's the top story."

"That is what I want to talk to you about."

"I'm not changing my mind about dating you."

"That is good to hear. I am with my speech writer, and I wanted to see what you think of the official statement that will be released."

"Okay let's hear it."

"It is with immense pleasure to announce that Her Royal Highness, Princess Edelgard Zelda Boru is in a relationship as of a number of days ago. This has been signified by Her Highness's Royal Claddagh Ring on her right ring finger being turned towards her heart. Her Highness is asking for privacy from everyone with regards to her new same-sex relationship. Her Highness will introduce her girlfriend to the people of Hibernia and the World during the celebration for all heroes which will be happening in a week's time, with further details on the event to follow later. Her Highness is hoping that the people of Hibernia will be supportive of both her relationship and her girlfriend.

That is what we have written. We haven't decided whether I will actually do the announcement or let either my parents or one of the staff do it. So, what do you think?"

"I have no problems with it. I would suggest that you do it, given it is your announcement."

"An excellent point. You better be watching when I make the announce then. It will be at six p.m. tonight. I am also going to email you the current plans for the hero celebrations. You should get them within the hour."

"Okay, I can't wait."

"I cannot wait either. Though I am already regretting waiting a week before we can tell everyone."

"Well, it will allow us to have some more time to ourselves."

"That is true. I wonder though when we will be finishing the hero course."

"It is strange, maybe we'll learn next week."

"Perhaps, until then we can try and figure out ways of meeting up"

"Okay, send me a text, when you have sent the email."

"You really need to get Wi-Fi for your home."

"That would require me getting a new phone or a laptop, which I can't afford and the school updating its internet policy."

"That is annoying. If you need any help, all you need to do is just ask."

"I'm not asking you for money and it would be wrong for me to get my girlfriend to influence the school's policies."

"I am just pointing out some options. Do not worry I will send a text when I send you the email."

The next day Circe headed into the City to spend some time with her friends. The Royal Relationship was still the talk of the country. As they met up, they began talking about the Royal Relationship.

"I can't believe they won't tell us who she's dating" Fiona said, annoyed.

"She has the right to privacy as much as anyone else," Yu said.

"Yeah, besides, she will be revealing her girlfriend at the big hero celebration. Speaking of which, you must be excited about that Circe?" Claire said.

"More nervous than anything else," Circe said, slightly embarrassed, "you know I don't like the attention."

"But you deserve it, though you did give us all quite a scare. I'm glad you managed to pull through," Yu said.

"So am I, it was a terrifying experience, but thankfully it is all over."

"Hey Circe, what's that on your finger?" Fiona said, noticing Circe's Claddagh ring.

"Is that a Claddagh Ring?" Yu asked quickly noticing the ring.

"Those are expensive right; how did you afford it?" Claire said, surprised.

"I didn't buy it. It was given to me by my dad, it's a family heirloom," Circe said, she didn't like lying to her friends, but she would apologise after the reveal.

"I see, though unless you are in a relationship, you are wearing it wrong," Claire said.

"I am? Dad didn't tell me how to wear it," Circe said.

She removed the ring and placed the heart pointing outwards before putting it back on. Though it was to prevent any further questions, it felt wrong.

"Still, it looks great," Fiona said, admiring the ring.

"So being the guest of honour, you must know what is being planned for the celebration" Claire asked.

"Not really, they are still making final details as far as I know."

The group of friends were walking and talking when the Puff Anders appeared before them.

"Well, what do we have here? Looks like some ladies about to part with their valuables," Sam said, threatening the four friends.

"Hey Sam, isn't that the girl who blasted us?" Nicki said, noticing Circe.

"Hey you're right. Looks like we can also get some payback."

"Stay behind me," Circe said to her friends.

"Circe, you aren't going to fight them?" Fiona asked scared.

"Athrú!" Circe said as she transformed into her costume. For her friends, this was the first time actually seeing it and they were impressed.

"You are going to need more than a change of clothes to stop us!" Sam said angrily.

The Puff Anders charged at Circe. Thanks to her training, she launched five short blasts at each of the thugs, knocking them out. Her friends couldn't believe it but were grateful. They quickly wanted photos of their friend in her costume and also started asking questions.

"Where does your costume come from?"

"What's it made off?"

"Do your clothes transform into your costume or does your costume replace your clothes?"

"Can you just take it off without changing back?"

"What's your costume made off?"

"Guys please all I know is that it appears when I need it and it helps with my powers. Alex did mention it was stab and bulletproof but that's all I know. Athrú!" Circe said as her costume disappeared.

"If it was stab proof, how did the villain stab you?" Fiona asked

"I wasn't wearing it when I was stabbed, and he bound and gagged me so I couldn't transform," Circe said uncomfortably remembering how helpless she was at the hands of Brendan.

"Sorry, I shouldn't have brought that up," Fiona said, realising she was upsetting her friend.

"It's fine. I'm safe and he's gone, so it's all good," Circe said.

The days quickly passed and soon it was the day of the hero celebration. Circe was nervous, not only was she the guest of honour but today was the day she was going to be revealed as Edelgard's girlfriend. The celebration would be taking place in Sunsport as it was her hometown, and it was where Brendan was defeated. She and all the other students were told by a text from Professor Fargo to be in full hero costume for the day.

"I wonder how Edelgard is going to pull being herself and Alex at the same time," Circe thought to herself as she looked at herself in full costume in the mirror.

"Are you ready?" her dad said, entering.

"Well as ready as I'll ever be," she said nervously.

"My little girl is growing up so fast," he said with a tear in his eye.

"Dad, don't start or I'll start crying."

"Do you have everything?"

"I think so, I just want to check one thing."

She reached for her right glove. She was wondering if she could remove her costume without saying the magic word and if her Claddagh ring would be there. The glove easily came off revealing her ring with the heart pointing inwards on her ring finger. Seeing her ring and how easy it was to remove the glove; she felt relieved.

"Now we know you can remove your costume if needed without transforming back," her dad said.

"I'm just glad, I'll be able to reveal my ring without depowering," Circe said.

The two headed out towards their car, where they were met by two Royal Guardsmen.

"Is everything okay, officers?" David asked concerned.

"There is no need to worry. Her Highness, Princess Edelgard, wanted to make sure you arrive safely to the celebration and to give Ms Goodwin this," One of the Guardsmen said, handing Circe a small device.

"What is it?" Circe asked confused.

"Just put it in your ear and then tap it and everything will be explained."

Circe did as the guardsman instructed. Suddenly a familiar voice came through the device.

"Splendid, you received the earpiece." Edelgard said.

"Edelgard?" Circe was a bit surprised. "Where are you?"

"Currently in Sunsport getting ready to watch the parade. You are wearing a secure psychic earpiece, so we can communicate privately until the reveal. It will also allow me to keep you updated on what is happening and visa-versa. All you have to do is think."

"Like this," Circe thought.

"Precisely, I hope my Guardsmen did not scare you."

"They were a bit of a surprise. By the way, how is Alex going to around if you are going to be watching the parade?" Circe asked as she also pointed to her earpiece to her dad, to show she was communicating with Edelgard.

"She should be arriving right now."

To Circe's surprise Alex in full armour flew above the castle and landed in front of her.

"Hi Circe, ready for the celebration," Alex said.

Circe and her dad were confused. How could Edelgard be apparently getting ready to watch the parade if she was standing in front of them as Alex. Alex deactivated her armour to reveal herself, though for Circe something was off.

"Allow me to introduce Ciara Dúbailte. She is my bodyguard who can also impersonate me if needed. She will be posing as Alex for today."

"I hope I will be able to perform as well as Her Highness as to not arouse suspicion," Ciara said.

As Circe quickly filled her dad in on everything. They all headed into town. Circe and 'Alex' met up with the other heroes for the parade, while the Royal Guardsmen took David to join the Royal Family in the V.I.P viewing box. Since he was the father of the Guest of Honour, it wouldn't be too surprising for the public to see him near the Royal Family. David seemed a bit uncomfortable sitting near so many important and famous people.

"There is no need to be nervous," Edelgard said to him, "Just relax and enjoy the parade."

"Sorry, Your Highness, I feel a bit out of place."

"Please do not. You are my guest, if anyone should be here, it is you. Besides the parade should be starting now."

Circe and 'Alex' met up with their fellow classmates along with the other heroes at the start of the Parade route. Circe was led to one float along with her fellow students. She was asked to stand on a raised platform on the float.

"Anyone want to trade places?" she asked nervously.

"It would be nice, but you're the guest of honour," 'Alex' said.

"Yeah, just enjoy it," Aoife said.

"I'm just not used to be the centre of attention."

"You'll do fine," Siobhán said, excited.

The parade began in earnest. The crowds gathered cheered all the heroes as they passed. Circe slowly began to enjoy it more.

"Are you enjoying the parade?" Edelgard said through her psychic earpiece.

"That's going to take some getting used to."

"You will in time, still you did not answer my question."

"I'm starting to enjoy it. It's strange having people call my name and cheer."

"You will get used to that in time. Nervous about our reveal?"

"A bit, but I'm not letting that bother me."

"Wonderful, you should be turning the corner very soon."

The parade turned the corner at Sunsport's famous round tower and arrived at City Hall where the VIP stand was. All the heroes bowed to the Royal Family and King Brian addressed everyone.

"Today, we show our thanks to all the brave heroes who defend our beloved nation. Time and time again, they make so many sacrifices be it psychical, emotional and mental, in order to keep us safe. We especially say thank you to the brave young heroes from Sunsport Super School who proved instrumental in stopping the Fomorian Brendan Ross. Your bravery is an example to all of us. As King of Hibernia, I would like to personally thank you."

The stage front opened up and a ramp extended towards the float with the young heroes. The Royal Family descended the ramp to the float and began to personally thank each of the young heroes. The Royal Family stopped beside Circe.

"Naturally, we have to say a huge Thank You to our Guest of Honour, the young hero who saved Hibernia from Brendan Ross; Ms Circe Goodwin!"

The whole crowd responded to King Brian's introduction with a wave of applause, cheers and screams. Circe still couldn't believe it was for her. When it all eventually quieted down, Professor Fargo joined the Royal Family from the VIP area on the float.

"Now I believe Professor Fargo of Sunsport Super School has an important announcement," King Brian said.

"Thank you, Your Majesty," Professor Fargo said as he bowed to the Royal Family. "Circe, Alex, Siobhan, Aoife, Patrick, Dermot and Declan. As young heroes in training, you would need to take a final exam in order to complete your basic training. However, it has been decided by the Royal Family, the Department of Superpowers and Heroics along with Sunsport Super School, that fighting and defeating a Fomorian Giant is more dangerous and challenging than any test. Therefore, it gives me immense pleasure to announce you have all graduated from the Basic Training course and are now one step closer to becoming professional heroes.

So, Your Majesties, Your Highness and everyone watching allow me to introduce; Alex Clúdach, Dermot McGrath, Siobhán Regan, Declan Walsh, Aoife McCarthy, Patrick Deasy and Circe Goodwin.

There was a massive round of applause at the introduction of the new heroes. Professor Fargo personally congratulated his students before returning to the VIP area. As he headed back to his seat, he stopped by David.

"You must be very proud of Circe," he said

"I'm always proud of her Professor," he said with a smile.

Back on the float, the young heroes and the Royal Family were ready for the next event as Princess Edelgard activated her own collapsible headset. King Brian and Queen Sarah stood back in order to allow their daughter the spotlight.

"Thank you once again to all of our wonderful heroes. Now down to some business. Today I promised to reveal the woman who stole my heart. Well, she did not just steal it, she saved it. My beloved is a hero, in fact she is her with me now."

The young heroes on the stage were surprised bar one.

"People of Sunsport, Hibernia and the world, I am delighted and humbled to introduce Ms Circe Goodwin as my beloved!" Edelgard said with delight as Circe removed her glove to reveal her Claddagh Ring.

Edelgard approached Circe and the two kissed. Cameras went crazy quickly followed by a round of applause.

"There's no turning back now" Edelgard whispered to Circe.

"Yeah, for both of us," Circe whispered back as the two waved to the crowds.

Indeed, there was no turning back. Circe's life had been changed forever. From an ordinary young lady to a hero and the lover of the Princess of Hibernia. Evil had been defeated and everything was right in her world. Except one question was still lingering in the back of her mind.

"Who was that female voice?"

The End... but it never ends...